All the paintings and sculptures in Rey's studio were of men

Naked men.

Marco muttered a curse. What had his brother got him into?

He actually flinched when Rey's silky hair brushed his shoulder, sending a rush of blood to his crotch. She had barely touched him, and already he was painfully erect. She couldn't miss seeing it.

"Marco, I think you'd be the perfect model for my new commission." She smiled, and he gulped. "Please take off your underwear so I can see the rest of your body." Her smile widened, two deep dimples creasing her cheeks.

How could he refuse? He hooked his thumbs under the waistband and pushed down his briefs. His erection sprang free. He forced himself to stand still and not look away in embarrassment.

Her sky-blue eyes widened. "Fantastic. You have the most beautiful body I've ever seen."

"Uh, th-thank you," Marco stammered. Who could have guessed? The blonde goddess loved his body. Maybe modelling wouldn't be so bad, after all.

Dear Reader,

My biggest challenge as a first-time author was digging deep into my creativity to make *Her Body of Work* a satisfying read. So to keep myself company in my artistic labours, I gave my heroine, sculptor Rey Martinson, the same challenge.

After years of hard work, Rey earns a prestigious commission to sculpt a nude male statue. But her self-doubts threaten to sink her until she picks the perfect model, sexy Marco Flores.

Marco is more than willing to help Rey rediscover her sensual, artistic side. But despite his sexual confidence, Marco has his own regrets. And even though he ends up baring all, he still manages to hide a huge secret from his new employer…for a while, at least.

How two lovers deal with their pasts to create a future together has always been one of my favourite themes. I hope you'll enjoy Rey and Marco's journey.

Happy reading!

Marie Donovan

PS I'd be delighted to hear from my readers. Visit www.mariedonovan.com to enter fun contests and learn more about my upcoming books.

HER BODY
OF WORK

BY
MARIE DONOVAN

MILLS & BOON®

To my husband, with love always.
Thank you for all your support.

First published in Great Britain 2007
by Harlequin Mills & Boon Limited, Eton House,
18-24 Paradise Road,
Richmond, Surrey TW9 1SR

© Marie Donovan 2005

ISBN: 978 0 263 85569 2

14-0407

Printed and bound in Spain
by Litografia Rosés S.A., Barcelona

1

CRAIG SPRAWLED NAKED IN front of Rey Martinson, asleep on the sheet-covered chaise longue. That was okay with her. She had worn him out, urging him into various positions and contortions during their long afternoon together.

His muscular back rose and fell with his deep breaths, his light brown curls pillowed on his folded forearms. Rey stood and stretched her cramped shoulders. She wasn't as tired as he was—but then, he'd done the hard work. She decided to finish while he slept.

After all, her male model was still on the clock, and the flesh-toned acrylic paints on her canvas were starting to dry.

Reaching for a half-empty tube of burnt sienna acrylic paint, she squeezed a blob onto her palette and worked it into the nearby blob of titanium white with her blunt-edged palette knife. A few more brushstrokes and she'd finish the painting in time to deliver it to her clients.

She cast her experienced eye over the contours of his back and buttocks. Her clients had commissioned a rendition of the ancient Greek myth of Narcissus—the young man who fell in love with his own reflection in a pool and pined away. Craig was the perfect Narcissus—handsome and vain, just like most men she'd met recently.

Since her last relationship had gone up in flames worthy of a Viking longboat funeral, Rey had spent the summer licking her wounds and the fall traipsing around to singles' nights and museum mixers with her best friend, Meg O'Malley.

Finally they'd both given up and decided to hibernate man-free for the winter. Meg was fighting for tenure at one of Chicago's snootiest universities and Rey had a bunch of art projects to finish, so their pent-up sexual energy could then be channeled into their work. That was the theory, anyway.

The phone rang. Craig muttered in his sleep. His bare flesh was covered in goose bumps. Rey hardly noticed the cold Chicago gusts blowing past her drafty loft windows but pulled a sheet up to his shoulders anyway. She crossed the paint-splattered concrete floor to check the caller ID to make sure it wasn't her mother.

Brigitte Martinson had been a professional wife all her adult life and still thought her only daughter's art career was just a peculiar way to spend her time until she married.

Fortunately it was her artist's rep, Evelyn, on the phone, who was probably checking on the painting in front of her.

Rey clipped on the cordless earpiece that freed her hands. "Hello?"

"Hi, Rey. It's Evelyn. How are you, dear?" While Evelyn Colby might sound like everyone's favorite grandmother, she locked on to business deals with the jaws of a pit bull.

"Just fine, Evelyn. In fact, I'm finishing that portrait

of Narcissus," she hinted, hop[ ] fore her paints dried into a har[ ]

"Glad to hear it, but I'm not c[ ] you sitting down?" Evelyn's usual[ ] an edge of excitement.

"Actually, I am." Rey settled on her [ ] She thought with an ample butt like hers the[ ] [ ]uld be more comfortable than it was. Hmm. S[ ]king of butts, the buttocks in her work-in-progress needed more definition. Maybe alizarin-crimson?

"You got the Stuart commission!" Evelyn crowed.

"The what?" Rey covered her palette with a plastic lid, resigned to another delay.

"I sent your portfolio out for review last fall and the Stuarts finally made a decision."

Rey sat up straight. "Do they want an oil painting or an acrylic?" Her loft building was being turned into condominiums. She needed a big chunk of cash for a mortgage down payment or else she'd have to move. No more twelve-foot windows. No more room for dozens of canvases and blocks of stone.

"Not a painting—a ten-foot marble sculpture for their new lakefront mansion," Evelyn explained.

Rey adjusted her earpiece. She couldn't possibly have heard right. "Did you say a ten-foot sculpture?" Although she made somewhat of a living with painting, sculpting was her favorite.

Evelyn rustled some papers. "My notes say Carrara marble, no less. It's being sent from the Italian quarry as we speak."

Rey gasped. "Oh, my God! Who can afford a ten-foot block of Carrara marble?"

Stuart family can. And what's more, they can
ord to pay you to sculpt it."

"How much are they willing to pay?" Anticipation
curled in Rey's stomach. Maybe she wouldn't have to
lose her loft.

Evelyn triumphantly named the fee.

The paintbrush fell from Rey's nerveless fingers,
splattering dark brown paint on her bare toes. "That's
six figures!"

Her agent was understandably smug. "That's right,
kiddo. You've hit the big time."

Rey's knees were too weak to balance on her stool.
She staggered over to the chaise longue and plopped
down next to Craig. He lifted his head and smiled at her.

"Hey, baby." He wrapped an arm around her waist.
She shoved it away and concentrated on Evelyn's incredible news.

"Am I interrupting something?" Evelyn had the hearing of a bat.

Rey frowned at Craig, who rolled over onto his back
and stretched both arms over his head. "No, that's just
my model. Tell me about the ten-foot statue. Where on
earth do these people live?"

"Didn't you read the society column I faxed you?"
Evelyn made a tsking noise.

"Sorry, Evelyn. I've been working twelve-hour days
and haven't had a chance," Rey fibbed. She found the
ingredient list on her paint-thinner can more interesting
to read than the Chicago society pages. Fifteen years of
hearing her mother gloat over them at the breakfast table had been enough. *Mr. and Mrs. Hans Martinson of
the Swedish consulate of Chicago hosted last night's ga-*

la benefit for the preservation of the Scandinavian spotted puffin, blah, blah, blah...

Evelyn interrupted Rey's trip-and-fall down memory lane. "*I* read them, and they reported that Mr. and Mrs. Preston Stuart III sold their Gold Coast penthouse and bought a lakefront home just north of the city. It's already a mansion, and they're making it even bigger."

"How did they pick me?" It was still too much for Rey to absorb.

"The Stuarts love the art and culture of ancient Greece and Rome. Remember the fountain of water nymphs you sculpted last year?"

"Sure, that was a great project." She'd carved the nymphs' faces to look like the owner's wife and daughters. It was a good thing they'd all been attractive women.

"I sent them a portfolio containing photos of the fountain and some of your recent paintings. They loved your Greco-Roman works."

"Really?" Giddiness swirled through her. She'd spent almost a decade watching so-called artists get grants for dipping themselves in chocolate or making sculptures out of empty toilet-paper rolls. Now it was her turn to show the art world what she could do. To show her parents and all their stuck-up friends that her painting and sculpting commanded respect. And lots of money. They all understood money extremely well.

"You'll get to sculpt that block of Italian marble into Mars, the Roman god of war. Totally nude, no fig leaf or loincloth. And if they like your preliminary sketches, they want you to paint murals in the grand rotunda. For an additional fee, of course." Her agent laughed.

"Evelyn, I don't know what to say." Rey blinked to keep the tears from spilling onto her cheeks. "Thank you so much."

"You might not thank me when I tell you the time frame on this project. The preliminary sketches are due in three weeks, so call that modeling agency. Pick someone who looks like the god of war." Evelyn's line clicked. "I'll fax you the contract, Rey. I've got another call coming in. Congratulations!"

"Wait!" But Evelyn had already hung up. Three weeks for sketches on the most important project of her career? Rey drummed her fingers, smearing light brown paint on the sheet. She had to call Meg. Meg would cheer for her and keep her from panicking.

"Good news?" Craig's voice startled her. She'd almost forgotten he was still there.

"Great news." It was the best news of her career, if she found the perfect model. She examined Craig's pretty-boy features. God of war? More like god of wuss.

He propped himself on his side and peeled off the sheet, revealing his tanned, naked body. His tanned, naked, aroused body. "Want to celebrate with me?"

Rats. "Sorry, Craig. I make it a rule never to get involved with my models." She stood and put several feet of distance between them.

"Rey, baby, who would ever know?" He patted the expanse of chaise longue. "Plenty of room for two…" he wheedled.

She considered him. Was it time to break her rule? After all, he was buff, had all his own teeth and hair and was presumably heterosexual. It had been a long dry spell for her.

"And besides, who said anything about getting involved?" He smirked at her, running his hand down his chest to cup his erection.

Okay, it would have to be a much longer dry spell before she'd wet her whistle with a drip like him. That was all she needed at this critical point in her career—another male model like her ex-boyfriend Jack. He hadn't wasted any time in spreading nasty gossip to all his model buddies in the Chicago art scene. For months all the straight models she'd hired had expected a roll in the hay along with their paycheck, like some kind of sleazy 401(k).

She tossed Craig a ratty black bathrobe. "Get dressed, Craig. I'm finished."

"With the painting? Let me see." He jumped to his feet. She didn't know whether to be relieved or insulted at the speed with which he abandoned his sexual advances.

He stared at the canvas. "The muscles in my back are much more developed. And my hair has more golden highlights."

Rey rolled her eyes. "It's not supposed to be photo-realistic. Besides, the colors will look a bit different when the paints dry."

He smoothed his hair. "Oh, okay. I do look pretty spectacular in this painting."

Just like Narcissus, Craig loved himself the best. What else did she expect from a male model?

MARCO FLORES GLANCED UP and down the dim hall, straining to hear any unusual noise, like a round being chambered or a pistol being cocked. But only the sound of loud hip-hop music came from one apartment, mixing with the smell of Chinese food from another. The corridor remained empty, so he proceeded down the hall. Francisco's West Side apartment building was as seedy as usual.

Even using his investigative skills, Marco had a hard time keeping track of Francisco. He moved in and out of girlfriends' apartments at the blink of an eye and had lived in six different cities in the past eighteen months. This latest place belonged to one of his bartending buddies who had taken a cruise-ship job for the winter.

He knocked on his younger brother's reinforced-steel door. Five locks and a chain clicked open before Francisco's head popped into view. Marco picked up his garment bag and ducked into his brother's studio apartment.

"Hey, Francisco!" He grinned at his disgustingly handsome younger brother.

"You're a day early. Good thing you caught me. I just got home from a gig." Francisco's hair was slicked back into glistening black waves.

"Still doing the modeling?"

"It pays the bills, and they really seem to go for the hot-Cuban look here in the icy north." Francisco shut the door, fastening the line of locks. "I wasn't expecting you until tomorrow."

"I flew into Milwaukee and hopped the commuter train." He didn't mention the four plane changes under different names to evade pursuit. He didn't want to panic Francisco, so he'd told his younger brother a cock-and-bull story about needing to leave Miami for a few weeks because he'd accidentally slept with some mobster's girlfriend. Even a mob girlfriend sounded good at this point. He hadn't been with a woman in several months, afraid he would let his guard down during sex and say something he shouldn't.

"You should have let me pick you up."

"With what? Your bicycle?" Marco set down the garment bag and pulled his brother into an embrace, marveling at how his baby brother was now as tall as he was. Although six years separated them, they could almost pass for each other. Francisco's eyes were the color of Cuban espresso, whereas his own were hazel, courtesy of their fair-skinned Spanish grandmother.

"What's with the ringlets?" Francisco rubbed Marco's hair.

"Knock it off." Marco ducked away. "My hair's still shorter than yours, Miss Shirley Temple."

"Shirley Temple? Like those kiddie cocktails?" Francisco tended bar part-time at a nearby dance club.

"Never mind." Marco had always preferred to tame his curly hair with a severe cut, but later the longer, more casual style had fit his role as a soldier in the Rodríguez organization.

After all, when millions of dollars in Colombian cocaine passed through your hands on their way to eager American nostrils, there was no excuse to dress like a slob. Or worse, an underpaid undercover DEA agent whose boss had initially refused to pony up the taxpayers' money for expensive Italian suits and handmade leather shoes.

Once Marco had made it clear that if he didn't dress the part of a rising lieutenant in the cartel they'd be undressing him at the morgue, the purse strings loosened up in a hurry.

Now it was time to get back to who he really was. "If you have a clipper, I'll give myself a trim tomorrow."

Francisco gave him a cagey look. "You might want to hold off on the cut. That hair will keep you warm. The weather's supposed to fall below zero this week."

Marco took off his black leather coat and hung it in the tiny closet. "It wasn't so bad out there."

"Unseasonably warm. You can borrow my winter coat if you want. It's brand-new, 650-fill goose down."

"Thanks." Marco knew something was up. "Why won't *you* need it?"

"I have a favor to ask." Francisco gave him the winning grin that made the girls sigh and drop their panties.

"How much this time?" Marco reached for the large wad of cash in his pocket. Untraceable and anonymous to bribe Francisco to take a free, spur-of-the-moment vacation.

Marco's Family Tourism Agency. His motto was Get the Hell Out of Town and Don't Ask Any Questions. *Mamá* had already left on her honeymoon cruise with her new husband. She and Luis had originally planned a quick trip to Puerto Rico and the British Virgin Islands, but Marco had bought them a six-week cruise through the Mediterranean. He wanted them out of the Caribbean, away from Rodríguez's sphere of influence.

"I don't need your money. I need your body."

Marco quirked an eyebrow. "I usually hear that from the *señoritas,* not my brother."

"Gotta be careful with those hot chicks, *hermano.* If you'd found out she was already taken before you did the nasty, you wouldn't have to come to Chicago in January."

Marco shrugged sheepishly, inwardly pleased his brother had believed his cover story.

"Here's my problem." Francisco flopped onto a low couch with a wooden frame. "I met a casting agent when I was bartending last week. He got me a soap-opera audition."

"Congratulations!" Marco eased down on the couch next to his brother and stretched his legs. It had been a long thirty-six hours of travel.

"*Hope for Tomorrow* is a brand-new show filming in Los Angeles. The producers want to capitalize on the growing Hispanic audience, so they'll dub every episode into Spanish, as well, and sell it to the big Miami television networks. The casting agent said they're looking for a handsome, talented Latino leading man."

"At least they got the Latino part right." Marco elbowed his brother in the ribs. He stopped laughing when he saw Francisco's glum face. "So what's the problem?"

"I can't do it."

"I was just kidding, Francisco. You've got plenty of talent, and God knows the ladies think you're handsome." Marco shifted his weight to keep the wooden slats from digging into his back.

"I have a modeling appointment scheduled here in Chicago for the same time as my audition." Francisco ran his fingers through his hair and frowned at the hair gel on his palm. "My modeling agency will fire me if I cancel again. I can't afford to lose them."

His younger brother looked miserable. It was the perfect situation. "Go to L.A. and audition. I'll go to your appointment for you." It would get Francisco away from Chicago in case Rodríguez found him. As for himself, he could show up for the modeling thing, stand around looking brainless, then hightail it to his next hidey-hole.

"Really? I was hoping you'd offer." Francisco straightened and stared at his brother. "You'd actually go on a modeling appointment for me? You can pass for me with your longer haircut."

"Don't count on me getting the job for you," Marco warned. "I'm just holding your place until you get back from California."

Francisco leaped up from the torturous sofa and pulled Marco to his feet. "*Muchas gracias, hermano.* I owe you one." He slapped Marco on the back.

Marco grinned at him. "You owe me more than one. If anybody knew I was prancing down a runway, my reputation would be shot." Not to mention what Rodríguez would do if he saw his picture.

"It's not runway modeling. Some artist named Rey Martinson is looking for a model for one of his projects. Just show up, tell him you're Francisco Flores, and leave."

"That's it? It sounds easy." Marco didn't want to go audition for some guy, but it was a small price to pay for Francisco's safety.

"It *is* easy. Models get paid for looks, not brains." Francisco dragged a soft-sided suitcase out of his closet. "Go take a shower and relax. I have to decide what I'm going to pack for my audition. *Your* audition is tomorrow."

Marco headed to the tiny bathroom. "Ah, the actor's life is a rough life. Since you don't want this artist to hire me, I won't worry about what to wear."

He closed the door but not before Francisco said, "Believe me, your clothes won't make a difference."

2

MARCO CRANED HIS NECK TO double-check the address on the loft building in Chicago's North Side Bucktown neighborhood. *Dios mío,* it was cold. The icy wind blew a crushed paper cup along the salt-crusted sidewalk. He pulled up his collar in case anyone was following him.

Francisco owed him big for this one. His younger brother had also left his fancy down coat at the cleaners and it wouldn't be ready until Monday, so Marco was stuck with his own thin leather coat. As he pressed the buzzer, blobs of dirty snow slid off the overhang and slipped down his neck. A string of curses burst from his lips.

The wide steel door slid open. *¡Caray!* Although Marco definitely wasn't familiar with Nordic mythology, the tall blonde in front of him had to be the reincarnation of some winter goddess. Her long pale hair curved on her shoulders, framing a pink-and-white complexion. Ice-blue eyes sparkled from between light brown lashes.

"You must be Francisco. Come in and get warm." She reached out a paint-stained hand and tugged him inside. Her full breasts bounced gently under her light blue sweater.

She had called him Francisco. There was no way he wanted to hear his brother's name come out of her sexy mouth. "Actually I go by Marco."

"Oh, I probably misheard your agent. My name is Rey Martinson."

Rey? The blond goddess was the artist? She hustled him inside the foyer to a large loft space full of canvases, drop cloths and what looked like chisels and hammers. Gloomy afternoon light filtered in through the floor-to-ceiling windows lining a long redbrick wall. He craned his neck and saw a rumpled bed in the far corner of the loft.

"I'll hang up your coat so you can go change in the dressing room." She pointed to a small curtained cubicle next to a platform.

"Change?"

"So I can see if you'd be a good fit for my new project." She hustled off to adjust a camera tripod.

Francisco had told him this wasn't a fashion-modeling audition. He stood still for a second and decided to go along with whatever Rey wanted. He shut himself inside the drafty cubicle and shucked off his ice-crusted black jeans, cold fingers fumbling with the buttons on his short-sleeved black shirt. He looked for the outfit he was supposed to model but the only clothing was a ratty-looking bathrobe.

"Your agent said you've done life modeling before?" she asked.

"Sure, I've done it before," he answered. *Life modeling?* He'd briefly dated a chain-smoking artist who painted what she called "still lifes"—big ugly bowls of rotting fruit that were supposed to say something deep about the futility of existence or some garbage like that. Maybe Rey wanted him to hold a fruit bowl while she painted his picture.

"Oh, great. I always find experienced life models easier to work with." Her cheerful voice floated over the wall. Her English was very precise, with a slight lilt on the vowels—as if she'd grown up speaking two languages, as he had.

"Um, what do you want me to wear?" he finally had to ask.

"You are so funny." Her giggle made him smile, but he had no idea what the joke was. "Just put on the bathrobe."

The clothes must be hanging outside. He left on his black bikini briefs and tugged the well-worn black terry cloth around him. It gaped across his chest and skimmed the tops of his thighs.

Pulling at the robe one more time, he stepped out and almost bumped into her. She had stripped off her blue sweater and wore a tight white tank top. She was as smooth and pale as a marble statue.

She looked up from the digital camera in front of her. "Come stand on the platform and take off the robe."

What? Marco tried to examine her expression for some clue, but she had returned to fiddling with that damn camera. Remembering his younger brother's excitement to audition in L.A., he loosened the belt and dropped the robe. She circled him slowly, appraising his pecs and abs. Francisco actually got paid for this?

"Would you be willing to shave?"

He fingered the stubble on his jaw. Not wanting to get the job, he hadn't bothered to shave that day. "I thought the unkempt look was in now."

"Not your face, your chest. Most models actually wax their chests."

His stubbled chin nearly hit the floor. "Wax my chest?" He'd have to have a serious talk with his younger brother about what was and what was not acceptable for Cuban men to do.

She shrugged. "Or not. Your chest hair isn't so thick that I can't see your muscles underneath."

"Okay." He didn't know whether to be relieved or insulted. He jumped as her finger stroked his back. "You have quite a few scars. You must live an interesting life."

"I haven't always been a model." Hell, he'd only been one for about thirty seconds.

"You're a welcome change. Most male models are cookie-cutter pretty boys. But you—you have quite a unique look." He fought to stare straight ahead as her warm breath tickled the nape of his neck.

"I hope that's a good thing," Marco managed as he tried to control his hardening penis. Even though Francisco could be a pain, he didn't deserve to have his modeling career wrecked because his brother got a hard-on in front of the boss.

"It's a very good thing," she reassured him. "Seeing you has given me some great ideas for my newest commission."

"What kind of artwork do you do?" He hadn't seen any fruit bowls, so he might be spared from still lifes.

"All sorts—painting, photography and sculpture. My body of work has a definite unifying theme." She gestured to the expansive loft.

He looked around and saw something he hadn't noticed before. All the paintings and sculptures in Rey's studio were of men.

Naked men.

He muttered another Spanish curse that would have earned him a smack from his *mamá*. What had his brother gotten him into?

He actually flinched as her silky hair brushed his shoulder, sending a rush of blood to his cock. Rey had barely touched him and already he was painfully erect. She couldn't miss seeing it.

"Marco, I think you'd be the perfect model for my new commission." She smiled and he gulped. "Please take off your underwear so I can see the rest of your body." Her smile widened, two deep dimples creasing her apple-smooth cheeks.

How could he refuse? He hooked his thumbs under the silk waistband and pushed down his briefs. His erection sprang free. He forced himself to stand still and not look away in embarrassment.

Her sky-blue eyes widened. "Fantastic. You have the most beautiful body I've ever seen."

"Uh, thank you." A blond goddess loved his body. Modeling wasn't so bad, after all.

MARCO GRINNED AND REY couldn't help grinning back. She couldn't believe her luck in finding him. When the agency had sent over his head shot and tear sheets, she hadn't been terribly impressed. He had been handsome in the photos, but his features looked somewhat soft and unformed.

But in person—oh, my God—there was nothing soft about him. His cheekbones sliced across his face, forming a sharp *T* with his narrow, aristocratic nose. Piercing hazel eyes examined her with more shrewdness than she expected from an average model.

His black curls and caramel skin told her he had quite a bit of Spanish blood in him. He reminded her of a Renaissance Spanish angel, lean and intense with burning eyes.

His body was a sculptor's dream. Think Michelangelo's David with an erection. She itched to touch his textbook musculature, but that was a professional no-no. His abs and pecs rippled under his skin, which shone even in the dim winter sunlight. When she had looked at his back, she had seen his hard buttocks flexing under his tiny black briefs and she had barely been able to resist filling each hand with a perfect mound.

But the clincher to offering him the modeling gig was his impressive arousal. Long, thick and jutting out from a thatch of black curling hair, it was exactly what she needed—for her commission.

Not for herself. No more models. Their arousals didn't mean much. Most were so narcissistic that just the sight of their own naked body was enough to give them an erection. It didn't have anything to do with the person they were with.

On the other hand, Marco was enough to make her throw her rule out her twelve-foot-high windows.

She pulled back from that dangerous thought and focused on Marco's nude body. She could tell he was uncomfortable standing there fully aroused, but he refused to hide himself or look away from her scrutiny. He held his head high, silky black curls covering his finely shaped skull.

The green flecks in his eyes bored into hers, and her nipples tightened and swelled. He dropped his gaze to the soft white cotton of her thin tank top. His eyes darkened and his erection grew even thicker and longer. A warm trickle of moisture gathered between her thighs. She broke eye contact and stepped away from his tempting expanse of satin skin.

"We should go over the business details." The contracts and modeling release forms trembled in her hands.

His firm lips pulled into a slow smile, revealing even white teeth. Uh-oh. He'd noticed her sexual interest and lost his self-conscious manner.

"You can put your briefs on." It was a temporary attraction. Once she drew him for hours, his nakedness wouldn't affect her so much.

He bent over to pick up his underwear. "I make it a rule never to discuss business when I'm naked. I prefer to reserve that for pleasure." His eyes invited her to comment on his teasing statement.

"For me, naked men are only business," she said, avoiding his glance. He was a few feet away, and his woodsy cologne teased her nostrils.

"Too bad." He dangled the tiny black scrap of satin from his fingers, tempting her. "Maybe you haven't found the right naked man."

She gulped at his blatant offer, the hot flush rising on her skin.

His intense gaze dared her to look away from him. She couldn't. Somehow she had lost the upper hand

and was reacting to him as a woman instead of an artist. She wondered crazily if the painter Botticelli had lusted after the model for his Venus or if the sculptor Borghese had lusted after his Daphne.

His strong hands curled at his sides close to his erection. If he moved his hand slightly, he'd be able to cup himself. She wondered if his penis felt as magnificent as it looked—long, brown and hard. A thick vein throbbed along the shaft, making her clitoris throb in unison. As she watched, mesmerized by the blaze of lust filling her body, a shiny bead of fluid coated the tip of his penis. For one crazy moment she wanted to drop to her knees and taste the pearl droplet.

She had to force herself to turn to her papers, shuffling them unnecessarily. When she sneaked a glance at him, he'd pulled his briefs on, but his erection was still straining against the tight black satin.

She cleared her throat, trying to shift his attention to the modeling contract.

He smiled as if he saw through her tactic. "So what do you want to show me?" The gleam in his eyes gave away his true thoughts.

"The paperwork," she emphasized. "Your hourly and daily rates are specified here." She pointed to the money details. "I'll cut your agent a check on each of the dates listed."

"I got the job?" He sounded stunned.

"Yes. Don't you want it?" She'd never had a model refuse a job before.

"Well, I, uh, thought you needed to see a couple more guys, then you'd take a while to decide."

"No, I need you right away." She blushed at her unfortunate turn of phrase. "I'm on a very tight time frame, and your agent assured me you were free for the next few weeks."

He ran his fingers through his black curls. "I have some obligations they don't know about."

She was starting to lose her patience. "Are you taking the job or do I call your agency and tell them you turned me down and they should send someone else?"

"No." He yanked on the black robe. "I'll do it."

"Sign here." She shoved the papers at him.

He barely looked at the contract before signing it with a firm, slashing hand. "I hope this works out for both of us, Reina."

He thought her name was Reina? Ha. No such luck.

"Actually, I go by Rey." She gathered the papers. "Do you have any questions for me?"

"Why is such a beautiful woman using a man's name?" he asked.

"What?" Big deal, he thought she was beautiful. She'd heard that before from men. What they meant was, *Take off your clothes and have meaningless sex with me.*

"In Spanish, Rey means 'king' or is short for Reynaldo." He stared at her with his amber-flecked eyes. "Reina is a queen, a name for a royal beauty."

She shrugged. "Rey is a nickname—and not for Reina."

"What is it short for?"

She sighed. "I don't really like my name. It's Swedish and not very familiar to most people."

He waited.

"Rey is short for Freya." She dared him to make fun of her old-fashioned name.

"Freya." The Scandinavian word rolled off his tongue with a definite Spanish accent. She kind of liked the way he said it. "And what does Freya mean?"

Heat crept into her cheeks again. What was it about this man that made her blush so much? "Freya was a Norse goddess."

"Goddess of what?" He moved closer to her.

"Um, springtime." And love and fertility, but he definitely didn't need to know that. "And since it's nowhere near springtime, you can go get dressed if you're chilly." It was a lame attempt at changing the subject, but she had to get her sexy model dressed so she could regain her equilibrium.

"We're finished for today?" He looked disappointed.

"I have a meeting at my gallery in forty-five minutes, so we'll start Monday."

"I look forward to modeling for you," he assured her, sticking out his hand to seal their deal.

Rey stared at Marco's long brown fingers topped with neat square nails. She knew touching him would be a bad idea, but a handshake wouldn't hurt, would it? It would be rude to ignore his outstretched hand.

She placed her hand in his. Rubbing his thumb across her wrist, he turned a businesslike handshake into a caress. Her breathing quickened. For one crazy second she thought he was going to bend over and kiss her knuckles, like a Spanish pirate in the old Saturday afternoon black-and-white movies. She'd always loved those Spanish pirates.

Rey pulled her hand away and looked for a pen, pencil, jumbo-size kid's crayon—anything so she could start drawing and ignore that sensual glitter in his eye.

He grinned at her and ambled toward her tiny changing room, her black bathrobe slung over his arm. His buttocks flexed under the tight satin.

She found a soft charcoal stick and slashed blindly at a piece of scrap paper. She heard the curtain rattle closed and finally focused on her rough sketch. Oh, no. She'd drawn the thick, long lines of Marco's penis. The tiny muscles in her vagina clenched in response.

She ripped the tattletale sketch into confetti. Working on this commission would either make her reputation or drive her insane with lust. And she wasn't sure which outcome she wanted more.

TEN MINUTES LATER MARCO walked out of the cubicle, grimacing as his snow-damp pants stuck to his thighs. Although Rey had a few space heaters scattered around the loft, the high ceiling gobbled their small output. "Aren't you cold?"

"No, I'm used to it." She looked at his pitifully thin clothing. "Apparently you aren't."

"Not really." He didn't want to get into details of why he was in Chicago without a winter coat.

"I was born in Sweden and moved to Chicago when I was a kid, so I have a few tricks to get through a long, dark winter." She grabbed a blank sheet of paper from her worktable and clipped it to her easel.

Marco had already thought of several ways and several positions in which to spend winter with Rey, starting as soon as possible. "If you're not busy later, I'd like to take you to dinner. You can explain more about your project."

Her skilled fingers curled around the thick pencil and stroked it across the paper's pristine white surface. He leaned over her shoulder as she stood in front of her easel, her spicy cinnamon scent mingling with her own warm scent of woman. His shaft hardened again.

She looked up from her sketch, black charcoal smearing her long pale fingers and her long neck as she brushed aside a blond strand of hair. He tried to recognize the shape of his body in her drawing, but it looked like random squiggles.

"I'm busy tonight," Rey stated, turning to him with a pleasant look on her face before returning to her work.

"What about tomorrow?" He ought to know better, but it had been months since he'd been so attracted to a woman.

She set down her pencil and faced him. Her ice-blue eyes were frosty. "Marco, I'm paying you to model for me. As your employer, I shouldn't go out to dinner with you."

She said *shouldn't,* not *won't.* Maybe she had mixed feelings. "Sure, I understand."

"Good. You're the most suitable model I've seen for my project, and I'd hate to have any hard feelings between us." She gave him a smile. Despite her cool manner, a hot flush crept up her cheeks.

His brain realized she was being smart and probably just following her professional standards. But his body wanted to push aside her thin tank top and see if her breasts were as pale and smooth as the rest of her.

She cleared her throat, drawing his attention to the pulse fluttering at the base of her neck. Triumph rushed through him, and he stretched out to stroke the thrumming beat. His dark finger drew invisible circles against the white canvas of her neck. Instead of quelling it, his touch spurred her pulse to an even faster rhythm. She swayed into his delicate caress.

When she didn't knock his finger away, he was encouraged. He traced the elegant horizon of her collarbone, the strength of bone and flesh hidden under her soft skin arousing him even more. He skimmed over her shoulder with the pads of all four fingers. His breath hitched as he realized that she wasn't wearing a bra.

"Marco?" Her blue eyes weren't icy anymore.

"Yes?" Her nipples had peaked against the thin white cotton of her top, matching the heavy pulse of his erection against his zipper. Her glance dropped to the front of his jeans. She zoned in on his arousal, her breath quickening.

If he lowered his hand, the hard tip would brush his palm. He needed to roll her nipples between his fingers and his lips, pull on them with his teeth and tongue.

"What are you doing?" Her husky voice held no indignation, only curiosity.

He smiled despite the growing discomfort as his erection strained against his zipper. "You have a few charcoal smudges." Only on her throat, and nowhere near where he was touching, but she didn't need to know that. He contrived to look innocent as she glanced at his fingers diligently rubbing away invisible smears.

"I think you got them all," she said, trying to be ironic but instead sounding breathy and turned on.

He decided to press his luck and hooked his index finger under the thin ribbon holding up her tank top. "I missed one right here." He slid his finger down the ribbon to the seam above her nipple. She inhaled sharply, and the top of her bare breast swelled against his knuckle, its hard peak grazing his hand.

She stepped back abruptly, forcing him to release her shirt before he ripped it. Their eyes met and held, blazing blue tangling with hot hazel. She looked away first and strode over to her desk and opened her appointment book. "Can you come at ten on Monday?"

Yeah, he could *come* anytime she wanted him—now, tomorrow, the next day. "Sure."

"Great." She swallowed hard, her delicate throat throbbing.

Monday he'd make her forget she was paying him to get naked. In fact, he'd do it for free, out of the goodness of his heart.

"I'll see you at ten o'clock, Marco." She sped him to the door. He turned to say goodbye and saw the loft's thick door close in his face.

She wasn't as indifferent to him as she pretended. If his Nordic goddess needed some encouragement to thaw, then he'd apply some Cuban heat.

"WHERE IS MARCO FLORES?" Juan Carlos Rodríguez clicked a solid-gold cigar lighter with his manicured thumbnail and stared at the glittering expanse of Biscayne Bay sixty stories below. Tendrils of silence twined around the sumptuously furnished office as he rotated his massive cordovan leather chair to face his assistant, Gabriel. Gabriel, who had been suspicious of Flores since the beginning. Rodríguez had discounted it as jealousy, since Flores was not only an astute businessman but also willing to get his hands dirty, unlike Gabriel.

"The feds don't know where their key witness is. He disappeared from the safe house several days ago." Gabriel met his gaze without flinching. "Our *informador* hasn't been able to find him, either, *señor.*"

"How much do we pay this scum informant to pass us information?" Rodríguez opened his rosewood humidor and picked up a thick cigar. He held it to his nose and sniffed, more from habit than anything. The fumes from years of cooking cocaine and methamphetamines had ruined his sense of smell, much to his regret.

"Several thousand a month, if you include the cocaine," admitted Gabriel. "But he was able to discover that Marco Flores was his real name instead of the alias he used with us."

Rodríguez cut his cigar with tiny gold scissors and lit the cigar's cap, rotating it slowly. He let the flame equalize throughout the tip and took a puff. At least he could taste the tobacco. The Cuban cigar rollers had finally gotten his special blend correct. If only everything in his life were as perfect.

Rodríguez had seen Flores as a possible successor. Both Cuban, both self-made men, both ruthless in dealing with their enemies. Except the man he now called Flores had his ruthless streak aimed at an unexpected enemy: himself, Juan Carlos Rodríguez, *El Lobo.* The Wolf.

And like the wolf, he would track down his prey, despite the incompetence surrounding him.

"Why am I wasting my drugs and my money on this man that you hired? What *do* you know?"

The younger man shrugged uncomfortably. "We do know that Flores is no longer in town."

"And that narrows it down to the tiny part of the United States that lies north of Miami!" The drug lord blew a smoke ring, squinting at Gabriel through the haze. "My conspiracy trial starts in just over a month and Marco Flores knows enough to ruin the whole cartel."

If Flores were alive to testify, the Colombians had made it clear that their esteemed business associate Juan Carlos would not live to see the inside of a prison cell. "So tell your source to find Flores. If he can't, cut off the money. Then cut off the drugs. Then cut off his balls."

3

MARCO BOLTED UPRIGHT, his hands gripping an imaginary weapon, his stomach churning. It had been years since he'd dreamed about the raft, that miserable hunk of rotting wood and worn-out tires. He was still amazed it hadn't sunk and drowned them in the Florida Straits, the ninety miles of dangerous waters between Cuba and the Keys.

He ran a hand through his sweaty scalp. God, he hated his long hair. If he hadn't agreed to impersonate Francisco, he'd cut it with his brother's manicure scissors. It only reminded him of the scumbag he'd played in Rodríguez's organization. He gave a dry laugh. His baby brother wasn't the only actor in the family.

Marco lay down and grimaced as the futon frame dug into his neck. It reminded him of the time he'd been hit with a two-by-four on a previous sting in Tampa.

He'd fallen asleep last night watching some action flick dubbed into Spanish. One glance at the clock and he groaned. It was already close to eleven in the morning. He swung his legs off the wooden torture device and stood. He couldn't believe how rotten he felt. The stress from the past year had finally caught up to him, and his body was paying the dues.

He padded into his brother's kitchenette to scrape together some Cuban-style coffee. He prowled through both cabinets, finally finding a half-empty bag in the freezer. Inhaling deeply, he smiled. The scent of the finely ground Jamaican blend made him homesick for the coffee stands on the streets of Miami.

He pushed away thoughts of home and measured several scoops into the froufrou German coffeemaker. The slightly burned odor of the liquid dribbling into the pot made Marco start to feel better. He opened the fridge to find some milk for his *café con leche*. It was nearly empty, no dairy products of any kind. Maybe there was some nondairy creamer.

He pulled out a five-pound can of protein powder. Ugh. The label guaranteed maximum increase in muscle. What was wrong with weight lifting?

The fine print read, "With a minimum of sexual side effects." *¡Caramba!* He threw the can into the fridge and checked his fingers to make sure the protein powder hadn't leaked.

Francisco's *pene* was going to shrivel up and fall off if he wasn't careful with his crazy supplements.

He poured himself a big cup of brew and dumped in some powdered creamer and sugar from dusty containers. He'd found a couple of stale almond biscotti next to the creamer, probably leftover from their *mamá*'s trip to Chicago last summer. Once the biscotti were dunked in his *café con leche,* they were somewhat edible. He stared out the kitchen window at the steel-gray sky. He'd better lay in supplies before he got snowed in and had to resort to eating Francisco's Amazing Penis-Shrinking Powder.

By the time he'd finished his skimpy breakfast, it was

almost noon, ten o'clock in L.A. Francisco might have dragged his ass out of bed by now.

Marco grabbed the phone and dialed his brother's cell phone number.

"Yeah?" a voice crackled.

"Francisco, is that you?"

"Hey, Marco, how's the Windy City treating you?" His younger brother's carefree voice floated back to him.

"If it gets any colder, my *cojones* are going to freeze off." Marco was wearing a T-shirt, a long-sleeved thermal Henley and a woolen ski sweater to top it all off and he still couldn't get warm.

"Too bad you're not here in L.A. I'm sitting on the beach, where the ocean breezes are cool and the blondes are hot."

Marco rolled his eyes. "I'm only here in Chicago because you begged me to take your modeling job."

"Correction—I begged you to go audition. Did you actually get offered the gig?"

"Yeah." Despite showing up unshaven, half-frozen and scruffy-looking as possible.

"And you're gonna do it? For me?" Francisco sniffled melodramatically. "I'm really touched."

Marco grimaced. If he skipped out, Rey would blackball Francisco with his agency. On the other hand, Marco couldn't stay in Chicago very long. Francisco had moved around a lot over the past few years but wasn't impossible to track. And if they found Francisco's place, they'd find Marco.

"Seriously, this is great for my career. My agent told me Rey Martinson is one of Chicago's up-and-coming artists. The Museum of Contemporary Art is considering a small-scale exhibit of his work next year. Any model would be thrilled to work for him."

"First of all, Rey Martinson is not a 'him'." Rey could never be mistaken for a man, not with her silky golden hair and plump breasts.

"Really? Just shows how much I pay attention to my modeling agent. If I land this soap-opera role, I'm firing her."

"You *should* fire her." Marco ran a hand through his tangled curls. "*Hermanito,* do you know what life modeling is?"

"I know what life modeling is. Don't you?" Francisco was uncharacteristically cagey.

"I do now, Francisco!" Just remembering standing nude in front of Rey sent a rush of blood to his penis.

"You mean this modeling gig is nude modeling?" His brother let out a shout of laughter loud enough to be heard in Chicago without using the phone. "Were you rough, tough and in the buff?"

"It's not funny, Francisco!"

While Francisco choked with laughter, Marco contemplated choking his brother.

Francisco finally caught his breath. "I swear, *hermano,* my agent never told me I'd have to go full monty. I wouldn't have sent you to take my place if I'd known it was nude modeling."

"Thanks, Francisco. I didn't think you'd set me up for this on purpose." He knew Francisco wouldn't have left him there hanging. Literally.

"Yeah, I would have taken the gig myself. The last nude modeling job I took, they paid me an extra fifty percent!"

Marco groaned. "I don't want to know the details."

"How much is this artist paying us, Marco?"

"Us? Last time I checked, it was my bare body on display."

"Whatever." Marco pictured his brother's dismissal of the situation. "How much, Marco?" Francisco persisted.

He gave up trying to make his brother understand and named the amount Rey had offered.

"Hmm. Not bad, minus fifteen percent for my agent. You can keep whatever you make," Francisco offered, obviously impressed at his own largesse.

"Muchas gracias." Marco's voice was heavy with sarcasm, which his brother chose to ignore.

"De nada. And Rey Martinson is a woman?" Francisco asked, still intent on ferreting out all the salacious details.

"Definitely."

"What does she look like? Is she hot?"

Marco shifted, glad that his brother couldn't see what must have been a goofy expression on his face. "She's tall, blond and blue-eyed." He didn't want to elaborate further. Francisco had a dirty enough mind without hearing how sexy Rey was.

"Tall, blond and blue-eyed? Damn, some guys get all the luck. Last time I modeled nude for a wrinkly little woman who chased me around her studio."

"So that's how you made your extra fifty percent." Marco knew the modeling world was crazy, but his brother always found the real lunatics.

"That old broad only got to look, no touching allowed. I've got my pride, you know."

Marco had his pride, too, but he wasn't sure how long

he could keep any pride around Rey. Standing naked in front of her, he'd almost begged her to wrap her long artist's fingers around his hard shaft.

His brother broke into his lascivious thoughts. "Much as I'd love to come to pose naked for your hot blond artist, I have to stay in L.A. for a while. I made the first cut and got called back for a second audition."

"That's great! Stay there as long as you want." The longer the better. "If you run low on cash, I'll send you some."

"Wow, you must really want this artist all to yourself. I haven't heard you so worked up over a woman since you went all the way with your junior prom date."

"No, it's not like that, Francisco." He wanted Francisco safe, and modeling was a small price to pay.

His brother laughed. "Sure it's like that. Anyway, I'll be out here for a while. The executive producer is in Mexico for an experimental face-lift procedure. The FDA banned it after a bunch of people wound up unable to blink."

Marco grimaced. "She must be some kind of hag."

"Actually the executive producer is a man."

Marco rolled his eyes. The man probably had a droopy dick to match his droopy eyelids. And Marco's own undroopy dick was causing him problems. "I know it may confuse your oversexed little mind, but Rey doesn't date her models." He was surprised to hear the plaintive note in his voice.

"She doesn't like men," Francisco commiserated. "Too bad. It happens a lot in the artsy-fartsy set. I knew this gay painter once who painted nothing but female nudes. Of course, he did have issues with his *mamá*...."

"Francisco." Marco ground his jaw, molars scraping off a layer of tooth enamel.

"On the other hand, lesbians usually don't go for naked men, artistically or otherwise. They tend to paint weird pink flowers or oysters, if you get my drift."

"Francisco." Mercifully his younger brother's attempt at Freudian analysis and art criticism meandered to a halt. Marco took a deep breath and began again. "Francisco, Rey likes men. She paints men. I think she even dates men. But she won't date me because I'm her model."

His brother's hoot of laughter nearly broke his eardrum. "She probably doesn't date her male models because most of *them* date men."

"Oh." Marco's conservative *cubano* upbringing made a rare appearance and he shuddered.

"Look at it this way, Marco," his brother offered in a conciliatory tone. "Show up, take off your clothes and maybe your impressive body will convince her to change her mind about dating her models."

Marco considered his brother's advice. "Actually, that's not a bad idea."

"I do have good ideas now and then." Francisco's tone became concerned. "Are you doing okay, Marco? Have you been spotted by any men with large necks intent on avenging their slutty girlfriend's honor?"

Marco stopped thinking about posing nude and got serious. "No, Chicago's the perfect city for me to hang out. It's big enough to get lost in, and I can cover my face with a scarf when I leave the apartment. Hell, I need to use a scarf anyway. Besides," he prevaricated, "I only slept with that mob chick once, and nobody with any sense would leave Miami this time of year."

"All right." His brother sounded relieved. "Wish me luck, and you'll see me next on *Hope for Tomorrow*."

"Good luck, *hermanito. Adiós*."

"*Adiós, hermano*." Francisco clicked off his phone.

Marco hung up and stared at the off-white apartment walls. He had refused to hide in the feds' safe house after one of his informants disappeared. No doubt the man had provided a meal for the bull sharks off the Florida coast.

Marco'd suspected for a while that Rodríguez had a mole, a snitch in the Miami division. Since he didn't know who to trust at DEA, he would trust the only man he could count on: himself.

Being turned into shark chow held no appeal, but neither did sitting around a government-owned shack on the edge of a swamp, watching satellite soccer and skin flicks waiting for someone to put a bullet in the back of his head. If Rodríguez wanted him dead, by God, that son of a bitch would have to work for it.

But damned if he was going to sacrifice Francisco. Marco would keep his younger brother out of town if he had to pay him. Considering Francisco's spotty income from modeling and bartending, it would be an offer he couldn't refuse.

He stared at the snow falling past the window. Chicago was cold, but it was better than being cold and dead in sunny Miami.

4

REY HUNG UP A NEW midnight-blue bathrobe in her changing cubicle and tossed the old bathrobe on her pile of painting rags. Marco had almost burst out of the threadbare black fabric. Of course, his chest and abs were much more muscular and well-defined than her last model. She stroked the pliant blue terry cloth. It would be soft and supple against his smooth skin. Lucky robe. It would touch him. She wouldn't.

Why, oh, why couldn't she find a nice, normal man who thought Monet was the French word for cash and Jackson Pollock was just an inexpensive whitefish from Mississippi? Starting with Stefan the Slug, her first lover, and culminating with Jack the Jag-off, Rey had gone for the dark, dangerous type. Of course, ten years later Stefan was mostly gray and about as dangerous as a set of children's finger paints. And as for Jack, the only dangerous part of him was his flapping mouth.

Rey shook her head. Instead of mooning over a model with an overdeveloped ego and an underdeveloped brain, she needed to get her art supplies ready. Walking to her large angled sketching table, she opened a new box of charcoal sticks. She was testing them on a paper scrap when her phone rang.

She answered the phone. "Rey Martinson."

"Hello, Rey. It's Evelyn."

"Good news, Evelyn. I found the perfect model and he starts today."

"I have some good news, too. I just faxed the contract for the male nude sculpture to the Stuarts' attorney. He called and said everything is in order."

Rey whooshed a silent sigh of relief. Her biggest commission was in her grasp. "You know how much this means to me, Evelyn."

"That's what I wanted to talk to you about, Rey." Evelyn's voice lost some of its coziness. "The last two paintings you showed me aren't up to your usual high standards."

Rey's stomach flipped. "I'm not sure what you mean," she managed to say. Was Evelyn letting her go as a client? How could she work on this big commission with this hanging over her head?

"Your technique was great, but the emotion wasn't there. The paintings seemed a bit, well, dull."

That stung more than she expected. Years in the art world hadn't made her so thick-skinned after all. "Dull?" Rey heard a snap and looked down to find her charcoal stick cracked in two. She wiped her smeared fingers on an ochre-stained rag.

"I loved the color, but I couldn't *feel* your emotional connection with the subject."

Rey rolled her eyes. Her dislike of Craig must have spilled over into his portrait.

Evelyn continued, "I'm sending those two paintings back. Only your absolute best work goes on display."

"I agree." Maybe her friends at the gay bar needed some new artwork. If Craig had a fit, so much the better.

"The sculpture for the Stuarts' Roman bath is crucial to your career, Rey. How many modern artists get commissioned for a life-size marble statue? This might put you on the map. If we use this as a springboard to move away from the male nudes, you could be the next Glenna Goodacre."

Rey's stomach flipped. As always, Evelyn knew exactly which buttons to push. Glenna Goodacre was Rey's idol. The American artist had sculpted the Vietnam Women's Memorial on display at the Mall in Washington, D.C. "What do you suggest, Evelyn? I don't want to goof this up."

"In a word, dear, *passion.*"

"Passion?" Rey grimaced. "Passion for my artwork?"

Evelyn cleared her throat delicately. "Sometimes when an artist is concentrating on her career, certain things fall by the wayside. Like family, friends and other more, uh, personal relationships."

Like sex, Rey mentally translated.

Evelyn continued, "It might be a good idea to take a short break and recharge your batteries."

Rey didn't think Evelyn meant the batteries for the gadget in her nightstand. "I see."

"I hope I haven't hurt your feelings, Rey." Evelyn paused. "But if you don't produce a phenomenal piece of artwork for the Stuarts, I will have difficulties finding such prestigious and lucrative commissions for you."

Rey knew what that meant: screw this up and kiss your career goodbye. "Thanks for letting me know, Evelyn. You can count on me to do a great job."

"Thanks, dear. I'll let you get back to work." Evelyn hung up.

Rey stared out the window. Heavy gray snow clouds churned, further dampening her mood. The door buzzer sounded and she started. The adrenaline rush of starting a new project always made her jumpy. She refused to think that her nerves might be from seeing Marco again.

She crossed to the foyer, her comfortable shoes squeaking slightly on the cement floor. She stopped and consciously slowed her breathing, tugging open the heavy sliding door. Nanook of the North stood on her doorstep.

"Marco, is that you?" He was finally dressed for the cold weather, a heavy scarf covering his face. He even wore dark glasses despite the overcast day.

"In the flesh. Or soon to be in the flesh, right?"

Rey caught herself smiling at his joke before she put on her professional demeanor. He stomped the snow off his tan boots and walked inside. She closed the door and he pulled off his scarf and glasses, pushing back the hood on a chocolate-brown ski parka.

"I took your advice and dressed for the cold. I finally have some feeling in my fingers and toes." He tugged off his heavy gloves and unzipped his jacket.

"I'll take your coat." The Velcro on the hood stuck to his sweater, and without thinking she moved behind him to pull it loose.

He looked over his shoulder and smiled. "Eager to get to work?"

"You're a man of many layers," she quipped, fingering the ecru turtleneck collar under his heavy sweater.

"What do you mean?" His voice was casual but his

trapezius and deltoid muscles tightened over his shoulder blades. She realized she was still touching him and gripped his thick down coat with both hands.

"Layers of clothing. They keep you warmer." What did he think she meant? Something more personal?

"Right." His shoulders relaxed and he turned to face her. "I am a man of many layers of clothing just waiting to be peeled away." He was so close she saw the tiny black flecks of beard along the smooth skin of his cheeks.

Rey dug her fingers into the coat to keep from running them along the clean line of his jaw. Instead of distracting her, the leftover warmth of his body radiated from the slippery nylon lining.

She hung his coat on the coatrack and tucked his snowy gloves and scarf on the radiator to dry. "Would you like some coffee?" She walked toward the kitchen.

"Maybe later. I already had a few cups of jet fuel at home." He followed her, his tread silent on the concrete floor.

"Jet fuel?" She turned to look at him.

"Cuban coffee. Strong enough to power a jet engine."

"So you're Cuban." That explained his dark good looks and slight accent.

He looked as if he wanted to call back his words. "Yes."

"I was born in Sweden, but we moved to Chicago when I was twelve."

"I left Cuba when I was twelve, too," he admitted.

"Really? Twelve is such a hard age to leave your friends and come to a new country. I cried for a month. What was the biggest change for you?"

"What doesn't change when you move?" He shoved

his hands in his pockets and began looking at her art-work. "We should probably get started so you can get the best light, or whatever artists need."

"Oh. Sure." Rey glanced at the ceiling-to-floor win-dows along the north side of her loft. The snow was fall-ing thickly and had blocked the natural light. But if he didn't want to talk about Cuba, that was fine with her. She wasn't paying him to discuss painful memories with her. "Why don't you change in the cubicle again?"

He rattled the curtain closed, and she flipped on the new space heaters placed around the modeling dais.

"A new robe?" he called.

"Yes. Hopefully warmer and better-fitting for you."

"Thanks. I appreciate it." He sounded surprised, as if he'd received few kindnesses.

"No problem." She smoothed the sheet on the chaise longue and double-checked the batteries in her expen-sive digital camera. She flipped her large sketch pad to a clean page.

One space heater was too close to her drafting table. By the time she pulled it next to the modeling platform, its blast of hot air had overheated her. The wool sweat-er her mother had sent from Sweden was overkill.

Rey stripped off the prickly garment and tossed it on-to a pile of canvas drop cloths in the corner. That was better. Her red long-sleeved shirt was much cooler.

She reached up with both arms and twisted her hair off her damp neck into a bun on top of her head. Where was that hair clip? She rummaged one-handed on her drafting table.

"Are those for me?" Marco stood two feet in front of her.

"What?" She inadvertently looked at her nipples thrusting against the thin cotton of her shirt. She dropped her arms, but not before the gleam in his eyes gave him away.

"The space heaters. They're new."

Rey waved a hand dismissively and noticed charcoal smears on her fingers. "It's important for you to be comfortable. Warm muscles are suppler. You can assume more positions and hold them longer." Her cheeks heated as a variety of positions totally unrelated to art ran through her mind.

He smiled, the skin around his eyes crinkling. "What position do you like best?"

"It depends." He meant modeling positions, right?

"On what?" He padded closer.

"On what feels best. I mean, what looks best." She caught herself inhaling his clean citrus scent. He was entirely too close for her already shaky self-possession. She backed away several feet and stumbled into her drawing table.

"Careful." Marco's hands on her arms steadied her balance but did nothing to steady her nerves. How had he reached her so quickly? She hadn't even seen him move. "Did you hurt yourself?" He rubbed the tender skin in the crook of her elbows, thumbs coming achingly close to the curves of her breasts.

"No, I'm fine." Her breath came faster, the movement pressing the sides of her breasts against his hands. She froze, desperately wanting him to stop cupping her elbows and cup her breasts instead. Her nipples tightened only a few inches away from his hands.

His own breathing quickened, widening the brown V of skin between his lapels. He bent his glossy black head toward her, closing the distance between their lips. She gulped and ducked out of his arms, hurrying to the raised platform.

"Why don't we get started?" She was proud of her casual tone of voice.

"I thought we already did," he murmured but obediently followed her to the dais.

She didn't have a comeback for his innuendo, so she valiantly put on her Nordic-ice-princess persona that had frightened off several overly affectionate models. Of course, it was hard to be icy when the masculine equivalent of a blast furnace was mere inches away.

She stopped at the platform base, staring at her setup with newly carnal eyes. The low-slung chaise longue was as wide as a double bed. One corner rose into a padded backrest. She'd draped it with a pure white sheet to get the best color contrast possible.

The muscles in his calves and thighs flexed as he lowered himself to the chaise. He bounced slightly, his knees parting the terry cloth. Her stare traveled up his long thighs to the shadow between his legs. Was he wearing those tiny satin bikini briefs under his robe? Or nothing at all? He cleared his throat, and her startled gaze flew up to meet his amused one.

"Good springs. And very comfortable." He patted the chaise next to him, making enough room for her.

She wanted to sit next to him. There was even enough room for both of them to lie down, but...no! Rey perched several feet away. Her drawing stool wasn't nearly as welcoming as the cool white Egyptian-cotton sheet next to Marco, but it was much safer. He tipped his head, his eyes gleaming.

Rey looked away. She always chatted with the models before asking them to undress to ease any first-day-of-modeling tension. But now she couldn't think of what to say.

The weather stunk. So did all the Chicago professional sports teams. And somehow Marco didn't strike her as the type to agonize over lack of public funding for the fine arts. He just sat there waiting for her to say something.

She blurted, "The new robe fits well." *Too well,* she thought, cursing her impulse to throw away the old skimpy robe. No wide expanse of bare chest or glimpses of tight buttocks. On the other hand, if she wanted him naked, all she had to do was ask.

Rey hadn't been shy around male models since art school, and she wouldn't wimp out now. "Take off your robe." Her voice was huskier than she expected.

"I'm all yours, Reina." He stood and reached for the loose knot at his waist.

She gulped. All hers. Artistically speaking, of course.

5

MARCO UNTIED THE ROBE. Rey held her breath as the wedge of brown skin widened. His eyes never left hers as the lapels fell open, baring him below the waist. One question answered. He wasn't wearing briefs today. He shrugged the robe off his broad shoulders and dropped it on the floor. He stood naked in front of her, his topaz body a dark jewel against the crisp white linens.

Rey clutched the sides of her chair, cursing her own foolishness. A chunk of marble must have fallen on her head over the weekend, causing artistic amnesia. How else could she have dismissed the effect his naked body had on her? He had the perfect male silhouette—wide shoulders tapering to a taut waist. His tight buttocks capped the hard thighs she'd admired last Friday. And his arousal—it was even better than she remembered. She wanted his shaft against her damp center. He seemed to read her thoughts, because his hard cock bounced even higher, pointing to his navel.

No, she wasn't an amnesiac. She was a full-blown sadomasochist and had no one to blame but herself. Here stood the world's sexiest man and she couldn't lay a finger on him. Not unless she wanted to renew the gossip that had mercifully died away.

"What do you want, Reina?" His silky accent slipped over her frayed nerves.

"I want you." Her response slipped out, horrifying her. Would that be a Freudian slip or Freudian lingerie? "And why are you calling me Reina?"

"You are beautiful, like a queen. How does my queen want me?" He stepped closer to her.

"I mean, I want you to stand over here." For someone who lived her life visually, Marco was a masterpiece. The Sistine Chapel, Taj Mahal and the Louvre had nothing on him. The Washington Monument came pretty close though, she thought, choking back a hysterical laugh.

"Reina? Are you all right?" The concerned look in his eyes grounded her flight of fancy.

"Fine. I'm just thinking about how to pose you." She pulled a crate closer and covered it with a smaller sheet. "Stand here and put your right foot on the crate."

He followed her directions, the pose throwing his erection into full view.

She tamped down her surge of lust and reached for her charcoal. Staring slack-jawed at her model wouldn't pay the bills. "We're going to start with some short poses to warm you up, so twist slightly at the waist."

He twisted away from her.

"No, twist toward me. I need to see your chest." She sketched quickly, but he was already losing the pose. "You're moving a bit. Can you hold the pose longer?"

"Sure." He turned again but not into the right position. She set down her charcoal and walked over to help. As soon as her hands touched him, she faltered, forgetting how she wanted him to pose.

Under the slight sheen on his skin from the space heaters, she glided her hands over his sleekly muscled shoulders. Instead of moving him into position, she reached around to the strong triangles of his shoulder blades, curving the tips of her fingers over his back muscles into the deep valley of his spine.

"Rey." He murmured her name and reached for her.

She jumped away, yanking her hands off him. "Okay, um…" She took a deep breath, trying to forget how smooth his skin was. "Marco, move your shoulders a quarter turn toward me."

He stalked toward her. "I'd feel better if you showed me again with your hands."

That was her problem. If his body felt any better to her sensitive artist's hands, she'd have an orgasm from just touching him. His eyes had darkened, and his erection had gotten even larger. Not that she was staring or anything.

She wished she'd just given him verbal instructions. Or better yet, oral… She mentally slapped herself and stepped away.

"That looks fine, Marco." That was a lie and the truth at the same time. His pose looked awful, as if his torso were totally disconnected from his lower body. But his body, oh, that was still the most amazing sight she'd seen outside of an Italian art gallery.

Rey hurried to the safety of her easel and sketched the heavy muscle of his legs curving into his groin. She found herself stopping to stare inordinately at his erection, drawing its thick lines in great detail, curving the head and shading the heavy weight of his testicles dangling below.

She finally looked above his waist and grimaced. He'd bent his arms like a butler holding a tray, blocking the lines of his chest.

"Twist slightly at the waist."

Marco complied awkwardly. Rey snapped a photo and examined the camera's digital display. Something still didn't seem quite right. She decided to try again and pressed the button to erase the photo.

"Okay, Marco, turn a bit more. That's it. Look over your left shoulder." She peered through the camera's viewfinder and took another photo. She frowned at the new image. Marco seemed stiff, and not in a good way. "Let's take a break. I'll make some coffee while you put on your robe."

He straightened and put on the robe. She peeked at him. His muscles must have tightened during their modeling session because he stretched his torso, rolling his head around. He was much more relaxed without her directions.

She measured several scoops of Gevalia Swedish coffee and pondered Marco's awkwardness while modeling. His agent had assured her he was an experienced nude model, but Rey didn't believe it for a second. She'd been drawing male nudes since her teens, and Marco was not a professional model. Not a good one, anyway. He also didn't look much like his head-shot photo and tear sheets. They seemed to be a younger version of him.

Pouring some spring water into the coffeemaker, she thought of one possible explanation. If he'd been out of the modeling world for several years, he might be using old head shots and tear sheets until he got enough money for new photos. What had he done in the meantime?

She sighed. That was none of her business. Her business was to sculpt a ten-foot statue. But at this point her fabulous model resembled a block of marble more than a Roman god.

MARCO FLEXED HIS STIFF muscles, amazed at how difficult it was to hold a pose without twitching. He ran his hands through his hair, grimacing at the curly black tangles. What he wouldn't give for a pair of clippers. But his hair was the least of his problems.

He could tell Rey was disappointed in their first modeling session, but he was honestly trying his best. All the smart-ass comments he'd made to his younger brother about getting paid to stand around looking pretty had come back to bite him. The next time he saw Francisco he'd apologize for being such a jerk.

The coffee hissed and trickled into the carafe. Rey came around the corner from her kitchenette with two steaming cups and a plate of cookies. He groaned inwardly. The strained look on her face was a far cry from the steamy sensuality he'd seen in her gaze just a few hours ago. Of course, that was before she'd discovered what a crappy model he was.

He had to give her credit for good manners, though. He sure wouldn't bring cookies to a guy who was screwing up his career.

She set a mug of coffee and the cookie plate on a small table next to the platform. "Try these *pepparkakor* cookies. My mother sent them for Christmas. She and my father are spending the winter in Spain."

"She must be a great baker." He admired the heart-shaped brown cookies studded with round white sugar sprinkles.

"Hardly. The kitchen is the place where my mother gets cucumber slices for the bags under her eyes after a late evening out. These come from the Scandinavian bakery here in Chicago."

He bit into a crispy gingerbread cookie and saw crumbs sprinkle the front of his robe, like some old housebound geezer who needed a bib to keep from dribbling on his bathrobe.

Rey pulled a chair over to the table and sat. She sipped her coffee, a thoughtful look on her face. "Marco, when was the last time you modeled?"

"Um, why do you ask?" he replied, stalling for time to think of a plausible answer. He shifted in his chair to try to dislodge the crumbs stuck to his skin.

"You seem a bit stiff." She looked him straight in the eye. "Like you'd never done nude modeling before."

Oh, shit. Rule number one of lying: stick to the truth as closely as possible. "I modeled for a while," he lied, "then I worked in the import department of an international company." That part was true. Rey didn't need to know his import/export experience consisted of infiltrating Caribbean drug organizations.

"So why modeling?" Her brow furrowed. "Surely international business is much more stable than relying on modeling."

He stifled a grin. "Actually, international business is more volatile than you think. Delivery screwups, hurricanes, unreliable distributors. Add to that a boss who was hell to work for, and I had to quit." That was no joke. Rodríguez had personally sent several men straight to the devil, and Marco knew his name was next on the list.

Rey bit into a cookie thoughtfully, her straight white

teeth flashing. A tiny crumb fell into the hollow between her breasts. His tongue itched to lick it off her
smooth skin. He adjusted the robe over his unruly cock
before it gave him away. Rey was still deciding his fate.
No, not just his fate. His brother's fate. If the modeling
agency found out about their switch, Francisco would
never get another gig. "I'm sorry about this morning.
Like you said, I'm a bit stiff."

Rey leaning forward didn't help his stiffness. Her
thin red shirt had several buttons undone, revealing a
deep shadow between her breasts. As she reached for a
second cookie, the side of her arm pressed a round curve
of breast into view. He craned his neck to get a better
glimpse and she sat back quickly. He grabbed another
cookie as if that had been his plan all along.

"Marco, it's partly my fault. I usually like to get to know
my models before we start, but today I rushed you straight
into modeling." She was actually blushing under her
winter-pale skin. Had she been eager to see him naked?

"No, no, that's okay. I'm sure I can do better this afternoon." Now that he had the general idea of how to
pose, he wanted to impress her.

"We'll start over. I'll show you my plans for this
project." Rey didn't know about Marco, but she needed
a break from concentrating on his naked body. Even in
his awkwardness he was still heartbreakingly sexy. She
stood and walked over to her desk. "You've actually giv-
en me some great ideas for my new commission. If the
statue goes well, my clients want several paintings."

Marco stood, as well, quirking an eyebrow. "Who
would want a painting of me naked?"

"Actually, it's a fresco." He looked confused. For an

artist's model, he didn't know much about art. On the other hand, she only required him to stand around and look good, so she explained, "A fresco is like a mural, only painted into wet plaster. It's a technique used by the ancient Romans."

"I didn't think there was much of a market for that sort of thing anymore."

"My clients are Roman history buffs," she began.

"'Buff' is right," he muttered, glancing at the wedge of his chest showing under the gaping robe.

That clinched it. An experienced nude model would never be so self-conscious. "Aficionados, if you prefer. They bought an extremely expensive, extremely ugly home on Lake Michigan just north of the city and are renovating it."

"Making it more expensive and marginally less ugly," he said.

She smothered a laugh at his unexpected wit. If his brain was even close to matching his looks, she was in serious trouble. "As part of the redesign they're adding a Roman bath."

His eyebrows drew together either in disbelief or uncertainty, she couldn't tell which.

"A Roman bathhouse was an extremely complex structure, with hot and cold running water, designed not only for bathing but for exercise, socializing and conducting business. It was the golf course of its time," she explained.

"Yes, I do know what a Roman bath is." He sounded slightly offended. "What I don't know is why anyone would want to build one. Doesn't their fancy house already have hot and cold running water?"

"Well, yes, of course. The house has six bathrooms, all with standard plumbing. They want the Roman bath to be a conversation piece."

"So why are these people adding something they already have and don't need?" He sat on the stool and propped his feet on the rungs. She was amused to see him realize the robe wouldn't cover his groin. He fidgeted like a woman in a miniskirt trying to climb into an SUV.

Rey tore her glance away from his strong thighs flexing under the blue terry cloth, but not before an answering flare of desire lit his eyes. She pulled her thoughts away from his body and back to her work. "I never question a client's motives, Marco. I'm their artist, not their shrink."

"This must cost a bundle."

He was right. The materials alone cost more money than most people earned in ten years. Her fee would also give her a measure of security. "I'm not my client's financial planner, but as the founder of the biggest computer-chip manufacturing plant in the country, he won't bounce any checks to build his Roman bath."

"So they want naked men on their frescoes."

His ironic tone was beginning to irritate her. She wasn't some graffiti hack who only spray painted crude pictures of penises. The best artists in history had sculpted and painted the nude male form. Someday she might have even one-tenth their talent.

Besides, he was awfully judgmental for a man who was taking her money to stand around naked to pose for those paintings.

"No, not just naked men—although you will model for several of those portraits." She was gratified to see his smirk fade. Put that in your panpipe and smoke it, Mr. Model. "There'll be classical Roman scenes of gods and goddesses frolicking."

"Frolicking is good." His smirk had bounced back.

She hurriedly continued, "In addition to the fresco, they wanted me to sculpt a statue as the rotunda's centerpiece."

"The bath is big enough for a rotunda?"

So he did know about Roman baths. Maybe he'd studied architecture or history in school.

She unrolled a sheaf of blueprints onto her work-table and weighted the corners with a small chunk of white Carrara marble, two quart-size cans of paint and her favorite chisel. She absentmindedly ran her thumb over the blade before setting it down, noticing a nick on the tip. She'd have to sharpen it before she started carving the marble.

Marco came up behind her, startling her. She was glad she'd set down her chisel before she'd cut her finger. The warmth of his chest radiated onto her back. She made herself concentrate on pointing to the main architectural features. "The square entry hall opens into the large rotunda. That space will be a round room thirty feet in diameter topped by a dome three stories high."

Marco leaned forward to examine the blueprints, slipping his hand past her waist to rest against the sturdy wooden table edge. "Perfectly round and proportioned," he murmured, his moist breath tickling the sensitive curve of her ear.

"Perfect proportions were very important to the Romans," she replied, fighting to keep her voice steady.

"And still are—to their Latino descendants," he added, the side of his arm brushing the side of her left breast. She turned to examine his profile. Her nipple brushed against his inner forearm, sending a bolt of desire zinging straight to her center.

"I've always loved the long lines of their architecture. Especially the columns. Tall and thick enough to carry any weight riding on them." She wiggled covertly to ease the sudden ache between her thighs at the thought of riding his column.

He made a sound somewhere between a gasp and a groan.

Oh, my. She realized that she had wiggled her bottom straight into his groin. She froze, his cock rising in response to her nearness. This was not helping her resolve to keep her hands off him. He was already long and hard, jutting through the flap in his robe. His hand stroked the curve of her hip, squeezing and molding the firm flesh of her bottom.

His breath came hot and heavy on the nape of her neck. His robe had fallen open to his waist, and the hard curves of his chest pressed against her shoulders. She gave in to temptation and shimmied up and down, pressing against him. He dipped his head to her neck and licked her there, nipping at her with his teeth.

She turned and shoved the robe off his shoulders, baring him to the waist. The tie loosened and the robe fell to the floor, his magnificent body naked in front of her. This time she gave herself permission to touch him, running her hands over his lightly furred chest, teasing the flat male nipples there while his fast fingers made quick work of the tiny red buttons on the front of her shirt. At the glazed look in his eyes she was glad she'd worn her fancy red lace bra.

"Beautiful." He cupped her breasts in his hands, pushing the full mounds together and burying his face between them. The clean citrus scent of his silky curls mixed with musky male sweat made her knees weak. Perching her on her drawing stool, he nuzzled her heated skin. He seemed to know when that wasn't enough and pulled at her nipples, the lace's friction on the stiff peaks making her moan. He flicked open the front clasp of her bra, and her breasts spilled plump and heavy into his hands.

She moaned his name and pulled his face against her bare breasts, dying for him to ease the aching peaks. He licked one nipple with long, slow, wet strokes, rolling the other between his fingers.

"*Dios mío,* you have the most beautiful breasts I've ever seen." He traced a finger along the top curve of her breast. "You're so fair, I can see the blue veins under your skin. And your nipples, so pale pink." He thumbed each nipple, and she arched into his touch. "Have these breasts ever seen the sun?"

Rey shook her head.

"You should sunbathe outside sometime, tip your perfect nipples up to the sun. I'll rub cream over you so you don't burn." He caressed the sensitive skin of her breasts with smooth, sweeping strokes. "I know a private beach just south of Miami where we can be alone. I wouldn't want anyone else to see you."

Rey almost felt the sun's heat on her bare skin, smelled the ocean's salty tang crashing on the hot sand. She shut her eyes and swayed into him.

"I'll carry you naked into the water and let the waves wash over us as we make love." His sexy Cuban accent deepened and slipped over her like an ocean wave. He unbuttoned her jeans and slipped a finger inside the placket.

She clutched his shoulders and rotated her hips against his dizzying, exhilarating caress. She was so close to coming that a dim buzzing started in her head. She opened her eyes and realized it was the loft's buzzer. Oh, my God! What if it was Evelyn? She had wanted to meet Marco and had said she might stop by. Rey couldn't afford to let her agent see her fondling her male model before she'd even made one detailed sketch. "I have to answer that." Rey pulled herself away from Marco and hurried to the intercom, grabbing her shirt and buttoning it as she went.

"Yes?"

Fortunately it wasn't her agent. Her friend Meg's tinny voice came through the speaker. "It's me. I was in the neighborhood and thought you might want to get a bite to eat."

Marco spun her against the exposed brick wall and bit her earlobe. "Get rid of whoever that is and I'll let you get a bite of me." He clasped her fingers around his cock. It was marvelous—thin silky skin covering a long pillar of flesh. She stroked the thick, pliant head, marveling at its firmness.

Oh, she wouldn't bite him, but she'd lick him. Just as she'd wanted to do the first day she'd seen him naked. Which was the day she'd hired him. Which made him her employee. *Crap.*

"Tell her to go away." He backed her against the wall, magnificently naked. "Tell her you're working and you can't go." His erection pulsed against the wet junction of her thighs.

"Marco." She put her hands on his chest. Instead of pushing him away, her hands traced the whorls of black hair covering his copper-colored nipples. His smooth skin burned her fingertips and sent jolts of pleasure up her arms to her aching nipples. God, she wanted him. But it was happening too fast. She couldn't think with his hot, naked body pressing against her. She finally ducked away. "Go get dressed now."

His jaw clenched. She didn't blame him. She was sending him mixed messages, but she couldn't help it. He was her employee, not her boy toy.

"I'm opening the door. If you don't want my friend to see you, you should go get dressed." She stared over his lovely brown shoulder, refusing to look him in the eye.

"So what? The whole world is going to see my naked body when your statue goes on display." He pushed effortlessly away from the wall, his biceps swelling.

"That's what I'm paying you for." Her fingers fumbled over the tiny buttons on her shirt.

"You're the boss." He snapped off a salute and turned on his heel. Not bothering with the robe, he marched naked across the wide loft. The play of muscles in his firm buttocks fascinated her until the buzzer sounded again.

Damn! He wasn't supposed to be so sexy! She yanked open the door. Snowflakes blasted her overheated skin. She hoped Marco got an icy breeze on his bare ass.

Meg O'Malley stood on the doorstep, her green cat's eyes wide. "Who's that?"

Apparently Marco hadn't gone into the dressing

room yet. Meg craned her neck over Rey's shoulder. "I can't see," her friend complained.

Marco rattled the cubicle curtain closed. Meg gave a pout. "Spoilsport."

Rey realized she'd moved to block Meg's view. On purpose? That was stupid. As Marco said, the whole world would see him naked soon enough.

"It's about time you had some fun, Rey. Who's the hottie?"

"Marco. My new model." And nothing more.

"Is his front view as good as the back?"

"Even better." Oops. Good way to play it casual.

"Well, well." Meg gave her a narrow glance. "You're turning as red as that misbuttoned shirt."

Rey looked down and groaned. She'd missed a couple buttonholes in her hurry to answer the door.

"Bye-bye. You have much more interesting things to do than get lunch with me." Meg reached for the loft door handle.

"Don't go!" Rey fixed her buttons. "Nothing's happening."

"That's why I'm leaving. Something *should* happen."

Marco pushed out of the cubicle and Meg's jaw dropped. Rey couldn't blame her. Well, maybe a tiny bit.

He wore a heavy Irish sweater over tight brown pants. The creamy wool made his *café-au-lait* skin even warmer, and the toffee-colored pants matched his eyes. He looked as delicious as a caramel sundae, and Rey wanted to eat him up with a spoon.

He smiled when he saw her friend. "You must be Meg." He extended his hand. Meg took it eagerly, flipping her snow-dampened black hair off her face.

"Meg, this is Marco. He's modeling for the Stuart commission. Marco, my friend Meg O'Malley."

"A pleasure," Marco murmured, shaking Meg's hand.

Rey watched them sourly. Any more heat from Marco and her friend would melt into the puddle of snow at her feet.

"If I'm interrupting your work, I can go." Meg looked avidly between Rey and Marco.

"Do you want me to stay?" Marco's eyes bored into Rey's, and the throb between her thighs surged forward again. She wanted him to push her against the door. Hot, sweaty, open-me-up-and-take-me sex.

She teetered on the edge but regained a shred of balance. "We're finished for today." Meg grimaced but Rey ignored her. "Can you come tomorrow at ten?"

Marco retreated into his formal manners, but Rey still saw his golden gaze simmer. "I will see you then."

"Marco, would you like to join us for lunch?" Meg asked, obviously playing matchmaker.

"Some other time. I'm sure you and Rey have a lot to talk about." He shrugged on his down jacket and lifted his gloves and scarf off the radiator.

Rey followed him to the loft door. "Thank you for coming, Marco." She sounded like her mother after she hosted a high-society bash, but she couldn't exactly say a thank-you for fondling her. Although she'd loved it.

"Don't thank me yet, *corazón*," he whispered, tracing a finger along her cheek to the deep V-neck of her shirt. Her nipples instantly pushed against the soft fabric. "I'll let you thank me when you *come*, too."

His husky voice shot arrows of desire through Rey's overheated body. She leaned into his touch, but he pulled his finger away. She saw the gleam of triumph in his eyes as he turned to Meg. "Nice meeting you, Meg." He sauntered out the door, not flinching as the snow swirled around him.

Rey closed the door and swayed onto the cold metal doorjamb trying to slow her breathing.

"Holy moly." Meg flapped her hand to fan Rey's face. "Those eyes. I thought the two of you would burst into flames."

"Don't be silly. I'm not interested in him." Rey scraped herself together from the puddle she'd melted into.

"So can I have his phone number?" Meg asked.

Rey spun around to glare at her friend, who threw up her hands in mock surrender. "Down, girl. You've only confirmed my suspicions."

"Aren't you ready to go?" Rey grabbed her keys and tiny leather purse and opened the loft door.

"Want your coat?" Meg lifted the sky-blue parka off the coatrack, and Rey grabbed it.

"Let's walk to the diner." The arctic air *might* shock some sense into her, although she doubted it. Marco made her hot enough to walk to Wisconsin naked without feeling the chill.

"*Señor,* I HAVE NEW information about Marco Flores."

Rodríguez looked up from his humidor. "Tell me."

"Our source in DEA found some background on Flores. Basic facts and photos. His mother lives here in Miami, but we are still looking for his younger brother. Apparently he is a model or actor and moves frequently."

"Probably *un maricón*." Rodríguez didn't care for

homosexuals. Fidel had had it right in the sixties to jail them all.

Gabriel continued, "Flores was born in Havana thirty-two years ago, lived there until he turned twelve and his father died." Gabriel consulted the printout. "His mother fled with him and his six-year-old brother and they were picked up at sea by the Coast Guard. A typical Cuban refugee story."

"What year was that?" A germ of suspicion infected Rodríguez's thoughts.

His assistant checked. "It'll be exactly twenty years ago this March."

Rodríguez tossed the expensive cigar into the humidor and slammed the lid. He ignored Gabriel's startled expression. "Give me the photos." He flipped through the dossier and examined the faces.

"Ah, Flores's precious *mamá*." Still a lovely woman after all these years. Such a pity he hadn't been able to sample her charms on the raft.

His admiration for Flores grew. To nurture his hatred for twenty years and wreak vengeance at the most opportune moment. A truly worthy opponent. He looked up at his assistant. "Pay *Señora* Flores a visit and leave her a message."

"What should the message say?"

Rodríguez smiled. "Boom!"

6

"I DON'T KNOW WHY I LET you talk me into walking seven blocks in this weather." Meg slid into the red vinyl booth, peeling off her gloves and blowing on her fingertips.

The icy walk had done what Rey had hoped. It was impossible to think about hot, sweaty, Cuban-style sex when your nose hairs froze every time you inhaled. "I needed the exercise. Swedish women are genetically programmed to put on weight during winter. If the reindeer population goes extinct, we can live off the fat stored in our hips."

"Like you have a big butt any time of the year." Meg unbuttoned her jacket and tossed it on the bench. "Besides, we're eating at a low-fat, high-fiber, organic vegetarian café. Your body burns more calories digesting lunch than the food actually contains."

Rey unzipped her own parka and pressed her palms against her icy cheeks. "My mother always warned me about Swedish hips. The kind where you look like you're wearing riding breeches even when you're naked."

"Didn't you tell me that she had liposuction on her own saddlebags at that fat farm in Switzerland?"

Rey grinned. "That fat farm is a four-hundred-year-old spa frequented by the rich and genetically cursed. She wanted me to come along for moral support, but I had a painting to finish."

"So instead of doing mother-daughter liposuction, you decided to go Commodore Peary on me and haul my ass up to the North Pole." Meg looked around. "Where's the St. Bernard dog with the brandy cask on his collar?"

Rey scoffed. "In Sweden this would be a balmy spring day." Ice crystals battered the plate-glass window. Fortunately the café was warm and cozy. A Tiffany-inspired lamp shed a gentle glow over the fresh daisies sitting in a cobalt bud vase.

"Right. Well, I hope this little polar endurance test chilled you out." Meg flipped over the upside-down mug in the universal signal of "Give me coffee." The waiter ambled over with the coffeepot, the stained-glass lamp reflecting off his five diamond earrings.

Rey buried her face in the thick menu. Soy-based inks printed on recycled paper, of course. "Wonder what's on special today?"

"First a cup of coffee. Then some nice warm comfort food."

"I don't know what I have a taste for." At least, what she had a taste for wasn't on the menu.

Meg must have read her mind. "How about something hot and spicy? Maybe a mouthwatering south-of-the-border treat."

"Meg!" Rey was glad her cheeks were still red with cold. At least it hid her blush.

"What?" Meg raised her eyebrows. "You could use a long, thick, juicy burrito."

Rey didn't know whether to laugh or cry. "First of

all, Marco is not on my *menu*, he's on my payroll. Second, he's Cuban, and burritos are Mexican."

"Cuban? Oh, my. Steamy tropical nights, salsa dancing, Ricky Martin."

"I think Ricky's Puerto Rican."

"With a bonbon booty like his, Ricky could be a Martian for all I care." Meg fanned herself with the menu.

The waiter appeared to take their orders and offered a basket of whole-grain bread sticks. Meg's teasing notwithstanding, Rey chose three-bean chili with corn bread. Meg picked marinated tofu teriyaki stir-fry served over brown rice.

"Homesick?" Rey asked her friend.

"Maybe a little." Meg shrugged. She'd grown up in Japan, her father an American businessman, her mother Japanese.

Rey glanced out the window as another blast of sleet rattled the panes. "Not me. Winter in Chicago is bad enough. At least I get some daylight to paint by."

"Forget about daytime, how are your nighttimes going?" Meg leaned across the table.

"I turn on the lights and work some more."

Meg grimaced. "Same here. We're preparing a special Asian art exhibit to go on display soon. This is the first natural daylight I've seen since before Thanksgiving."

"How's work?" Rey asked. Meg had a Ph.D. in Asian art and was often asked to authenticate antique documents from Japan and China, her area of expertise.

"I think I might get tenure this spring. My creepy boss liked my last two published journal articles." Her friend grinned and bit into a bread stick.

"Congratulations! You've been slaving away long

enough." Considering Meg was fluent in Japanese, Mandarin Chinese and Cantonese, her promotion was long overdue.

"No kidding. You know the gloves we have to wear so we don't get skin oils on the scrolls and manuscripts? I forgot to take them off at the sub shop and didn't even notice until I picked up my sandwich. The waitress must have thought I had a germ phobia."

Rey laughed. "Once I was in the middle of a painting and ran to get a salad at the deli. The guy at the counter couldn't stop staring at my breasts."

The waiter served their salads. Judging from the rainbow pin on his shirt, he probably wasn't the type of guy to leer at women.

Meg rolled her eyes. "Don't complain to me. You'd need a magnifying glass to stare at my chest."

"I thought he was pretty rude until I got home and looked at my shirt. I had a blob of red paint over each nipple." To this day, the deli guy still winked at her.

"As if he wasn't going to stare anyway," her friend scoffed. "Was he cute?"

"Only if you like them sixty and sassy."

"Until Sean Connery comes to my door wearing nothing but a kilt, I'll stick with younger men." Meg's eyes widened and she slapped a hand over her mouth. "I'm sorry, Rey. I'll take my foot out of my mouth now."

Rey had confided in her friend about losing her virginity at age eighteen to forty-two-year-old Stefan Early. She waved a hand. "Stefan was a long time ago. I actually spotted him at a gallery exhibition last week."

"What?" Meg looked up from her plate, poised to eat a bite of salad.

"In the flesh. The wrinkly, pasty flesh." She hadn't tried to get a closer look.

Meg clattered her forkful of organic arugula against her plate. "Stefan Early? From what you told me, his name should have been Stefan Come-Early."

Rey giggled. "He did have a problem with, um, anticipation."

"Anticipation?" Meg grabbed a fat bread stick and drooped the tip downward. "That's a nice way of saying premature ejaculation."

"I was eighteen and didn't know any better." Rey drank some of her hot tea. Too bitter. She pulled a packet of herbal sweetener from the table rack.

Meg rolled her eyes. "And that's why Stefan is notorious for dating teenagers. An experienced woman would never tolerate such a lousy lover."

"He's recovered from his heart attack last year." Rey stirred the sweet powder into her tea.

"Is it true he collapsed on top of his nineteen-year-old girlfriend?" Meg asked.

"I heard that, too, but I don't believe it." Rey gave Meg a wicked smile. "How could five seconds of thrusting give anyone a heart attack?"

Meg whooped and fell back on the red vinyl booth. Rey smiled, but her heart wasn't really in it. She sipped her drink. The bitterness was gone from her tea but not her memories.

Her friend caught her breath and sat up. "I'm glad you can joke about him now. I wanted to strangle him with his greasy gray ponytail for how he treated you."

Rey'd never told Meg half of what Stefan had done, but now wasn't the time. She decided to lighten the mood, especially since the waiter was approaching with their lunch. "My first lover, but not the last."

"Thank God. You deserve a man with more staying power." Meg took a bite of the thick bread stick.

"Amen, honey." The waiter winked at them, leaning in to serve their plates with a flourish. "We all deserve that."

"See? Even our waiter agrees."

Rey pointed her fork across the table at her outrageous friend. "Use your mouth for eating instead of embarrassing me." She dug into her own meal.

Meg gave her an injured look. "Have I even mentioned that new model of yours?"

Caught with a mouthful of corn bread, Rey couldn't defend herself without spraying crumbs on the pretty blue-and-white-checked tablecloth.

"Did I even ask how you could be so crazy to have lunch with me instead of rolling around with a hot, naked man?" Meg sliced into her tofu and grimaced. "It's weird to eat Japanese food with a knife and fork."

Rey finally swallowed. "I don't have time to roll around naked with a man, much less my own model. If I goof up this commission, I'll have to move and Evelyn will drop me."

"I know your building's going condo, but why would Evelyn fire you?" Meg ate a bite of stir-fry.

Rey set down her spoon, her appetite waning. "She said my last few paintings were dull."

"Ouch. You're not a dull person, so what's going on?"

"She said I need more passion," Rey said glumly.

"Doesn't everyone?" Meg replied. "You've had a drier spell than most, though. How long has it been for you?"

"Passion in my artwork, not sex." She refused to think there was a connection.

"And you don't think the two are related?"

Busted. Rey shrugged.

"So Evelyn says you're missing some passion in your artwork." Meg leaned closer. "I think you need to get laid."

"Meg!" Rey shushed her friend and looked around the café to see if anyone had overheard their conversation. The waiter scurried over with a damp cloth and began wiping the salt and pepper shakers on the next table.

"It's perfect! Give in to your attraction for Marco. Passion for your model equals passion for your artwork."

"No, it doesn't work like that." Rey narrowed her gaze at the waiter. He was arranging the sweetener packets by color.

Meg gave her a skeptical look. "Come on now. I may be a bit rusty on my art history, but I can think of several artists who played Hide the Paintbrush with their models. Picasso?"

"Yes."

"That French sculptor, Rodin?"

"Yes." Actually one of her favorite sculptors, despite his horrible character.

"And no one can tell me Paul Gaugin had a purely artistic relationship with those topless South Sea beauties."

"Probably not."

"And no one thought any the less of those artists?"

"Well…it was a different century, and they were men." It sounded weak even to her.

Meg stuck out her tongue. "Why should male artists have all the fun?"

Rey sat up straight. "Maybe they shouldn't."

"Damn right." Meg pointed her fork at Rey. "And it's a business expense. Maybe you can write it off at tax time."

"Marco is not a gigolo!" By then the waiter had quit all pretense of work and openly listened.

Meg lowered her voice. "I know you're not going to pay him for sex. From what I saw, he'd gladly do you for free."

"Meg!" Rey grabbed her ice water and pressed the cold glass to her burning cheeks.

"Didn't you just take a seminar at the Art Institute on advanced methods of stone sculpture?" Her friend had a calculating look on her face.

"Yes, last month. So?" Rey picked up her glass and took a deep drink.

"Think of sex with Marco as a continuing-education course."

Rey giggled. "Passion 101."

"With those smoldering looks he was giving you, I think you'd get a graduate-level class." Meg sighed melodramatically. "Much more fun than comparing chiseling techniques."

"Hey, chisels are very important to me." Rey owned twenty-three, as a matter of fact.

Meg reached over and clasped her wrist. "Listen, Rey, if you screw up this statue, you can throw those chisels into Lake Michigan. You need to get it right any way you can."

Rey stared at her friend and knew she was right. Why was she kidding herself? Sex with Marco would be an enjoyable, educational experience. "I'd have to make sure he realized that his modeling and anything else we do are kept separate."

Her friend laughed. "You mean sex without strings? What man would pass on that?"

"True." Rey stared over her friend's shoulder. She caught the waiter's eye, who grinned and gave her a thumbs-up.

"Earth to Rey." Meg waved a hand. "Have you decided?"

Yes, she had. "I have to call my accountant."

"Your accountant? Why?"

"To see if lingerie is a tax-deductible business expense." Rey smiled at her friend, relief washing over her as she made her decision.

Meg flagged the waiter. Not hard to do, since he was eighteen inches away. "Two slices of carrot cake and a bottle of champagne." He trotted back to the kitchen.

"They serve liquor here?" Rey asked.

"Made with the finest organically grown grapes." Meg leaned in. "Don't worry—it still gives you the same buzz."

The waiter served two thick wedges of carrot cake on white stoneware plates garnished with candied orange peel and honey-roasted walnut halves. He poured the golden bubbly liquid into two champagne flutes and set the bottle on the table.

"Yum." Rey popped a nut into her mouth and crunched the delicious treat. Its mixture of saltiness and sweetness slipped over her tongue like Marco's smooth skin.

"Eat." Meg gestured with her forkful of cake. "You need your energy for your continuing-education class. When will you see Marco again?"

"Tomorrow morning." That was, if he didn't call her to quit after she'd given him the brush-off.

"No good. Call him and tell him you want to do an extra session tonight. If you wait until tomorrow, you'll chicken out."

"I won't chicken out."

"Prove it. Call him now."

"Now?"

"Here's my phone. You know his number, right?"

Rey had stared at his modeling contract long enough to know his home number by heart. She grabbed the cell phone and dialed. She looked at her friend. "It's ringing."

Marco's voice sounded different on his voice-mail message. She waited for the beep and took a deep breath. "Marco, it's Rey. I know it's short notice, but can you come by my studio tonight at eight? I, um…" She looked at Meg, who rotated her hand in a keep-going gesture.

"I wanted to do an evening session to get some sketches in artificial light, because the sculpture will be seen in all sorts of light—sunlight, fluorescent light-bulbs…" Meg made a slicing motion across her neck. It was time to stop babbling. "See you at eight."

She clicked off the phone and slumped in her seat.

Meg grinned at her. "As your guidance counselor, I'd like to thank you for registering for advanced studies in human sexuality."

"What if I flunk?" Rey doodled a frowny face in her frosting with her fork.

"You'll get an A-plus. Underneath your cool Nordic exterior beats the heart of a wild Viking maiden."

"Maiden?" Rey raised an eyebrow. "Not for a long time."

"Even better. I bet Marco wants a woman who knows

what she's doing." Meg raised her champagne flute. "A toast to passion, sex and passionate sex."

"Cheers." Rey tossed down her champagne. Maybe if the butterflies in her stomach got drunk enough, they'd stop fluttering around.

7

MARCO TURNED THE CORNER onto Rey's street, eager to see her again. The temperature had dropped into the low teens with nightfall, so no one on the bus had paid any attention to his heavily wrapped face.

Half a block from her loft he heard footsteps behind him. Marco waited until he got past a streetlight and ducked into a doorway. He reached slowly into his coat pocket and pulled out his pistol, flipping off the safety.

Whoever was following him came closer. Marco purposely slowed his breathing, his pulse slowing in response. He entered that hyperaware state that always accompanied danger, every muscle in his body readying for action.

A shadowy figure crossed the doorway. Marco's arm shot out, dragging his stalker into the dark alcove. He cut off the man's gasp with a forearm across the throat, showing him the pistol. "What do you want?" He gave the guy enough air to reply.

"Nothin', man. I swear!" His eyes widened with fright at the gun near his head.

"Nothing?" Marco shook him. "Why are you following me?"

"Man, I'm just tryin' to get to the shelter around the corner. I don't wanna freeze to death."

Marco let up the pressure on his throat and patted him down quickly. No weapons except for a pocketknife. Now that the initial surge of adrenaline had passed, he noticed the wind-chapped cheeks and the stale smell of booze emanating from the man's pores.

Unless Rodríguez had stooped to hiring winos as assassins, Marco had just mugged a local bum.

"Get lost." He shoved the guy out of the doorway before he got a good look at Marco. His victim needed no encouragement, dragging his two-wheeled shopping cart away as fast as he could.

Marco muttered a particularly vile Spanish curse. Just because that man had been innocent didn't mean the next man would be. He was both disturbed and gratified that his instincts hadn't dulled since he'd left the cartel.

He dropped his hand to his side, the pistol suddenly dead weight. The homeless guy was long gone, so Marco hurried to Rey's loft, shoving the pistol in his pocket.

She had sounded a bit strained in her message when she'd said something about wanting to see him in different kinds of light. He was surprised she'd even wanted to see him at all after their awkward parting. He'd been less than suave when she'd pulled away from their sexy embrace.

He tried to tell himself that he was only there to help his brother, but Rey's beautiful face kept popping into his mind. What the hell was he doing staying around? He'd made Francisco and their *mamá* as safe as he could. Now he was the only one in imminent danger.

Enough already. He uncocked the pistol and put the safety on before he zipped his pocket and pressed the buzzer. The loft door rattled open, startling him away from his surveillance. Rey stood silhouetted in the doorway, her long gauzy skirt almost transparent in the rectangle of warm yellow light. She wore a sky-blue silk shirt knotted at the waist, a slice of creamy white flesh peeping out. Her sleeves were rolled to her elbows and the top three buttons were undone, showing a generous cleavage.

His cock reacted instantly, pushing hard against his zipper. She had a full, womanly figure, unlike those skin-and-bones girls who were always chasing his brother around. Her full breasts narrowed into a tiny waist, flaring into rounded hips. Her luscious hourglass figure reminded him of the beautiful Cuban women of his adolescence.

She interrupted his lustful reverie. "Would you like to come in, Marco?"

Oh, yes, he would. "Thanks." Silently blessing the heavy winter coat for hiding his erection, he stepped inside and knocked the slush off his boots.

By the time he'd unlaced them, his arousal had subsided enough that he unzipped his coat without sporting wood.

"I'll hang up your coat for you."

"No, that's all right." She would wonder why his goose-down coat was so heavy, so he hung it up himself. Soft jazz music pulsed from hidden speakers and sweet-smelling candles added their perfume to the air.

"I like that color on you." She ran her hand along the dark green sleeve of his brother's cashmere sweater. "It feels good, too."

"Yes, it does." He covered her hand with his, enjoy-

ing the slightly callused strength of her fingers. They
were working hands, long and tapered, with short, neatly rounded nails. He flipped over her palm. "No charcoal smears this time."

She pulled her hand back. "I didn't want to smudge
my skirt."

"It's very nice." Sheer white to contrast with her thin
blue silk shirt and totally impractical for a long sketching session. Was it wishful thinking or did she have
something in mind besides art? He made a mental list
as he followed her into the kitchen, the skirt's long folds
clinging to her swaying hips.

Why it Was a Bad Idea to Get Involved with Rey.
Number one on the list was the possibility of a painful,
violent death for them both if Rodríguez caught him.
Number two was she seemed like a nice person and he
didn't want to screw her and then screw her over by
leaving suddenly. Somewhere at the bottom of the list
was a distant concern for Francisco's career, but his
brother was like a cat, always landing on his feet.

Marco usually did, too, but having nine lives would
be much more useful at this point.

"Would you like a drink?" She glided past an
L-shaped granite countertop with several stools. Two
long rows of light wood cabinets reached eight feet in
the air. Above them several small spotlights illuminat-
ed the exposed beams of the twelve-foot ceiling. Their
indirect light created a dim, intimate space.

"Sure. What do you have?"

She bent over to peer into the big stainless-steel refrigerator. "A nice bottle of Beaujolais, some California zinfandel." Her breasts swayed freely under the thin

silk, peeking from the unbuttoned V-neck. He'd bet his last meager paycheck from DEA that she wasn't wearing a bra.

"White is fine." He wasn't a big wine drinker, but his mouth had suddenly gone dry as he made a new mental list.

Why He Should Get Involved with Rey. Number one, she was sexy. Number two, she was seriously sexy. Number three, his balls would fall off if he didn't get to touch and lick her sexy body all over.

"Oh, and I have a couple different kinds of beer." He heard the clink of glass as she straightened triumphantly, a bottle in each hand. He ignored the beer and stared at her nipples. The cold air had stiffened them into ice-hard points. They pressed against her shirt, luring him to warm them with his tongue. A beautiful blonde with hard nipples holding two beer bottles. She was every man's fantasy. Desire surged strong and fierce, swelling his cock again.

She must have sensed the banked arousal in the room, because she bustled around, setting several bottles on the countertop. "If you don't like German beer, I have Guinness extra stout, pale ale and this Cuban beer."

"Hatuey beer?" The familiar sight of Cuban Miami's favorite beer gave Marco a pang of homesickness, distracting him from her lovely body. "I didn't know you could buy it in Chicago."

She smiled. "I saw it at the local liquor store and thought you might enjoy it."

"A little sip of home." He admired the red-and-gold stylized drawing of the Native Cuban chief Hatuey, who had fought against the Spanish conquistadors. Too bad there wasn't a modern Hatuey to rescue Cuba.

"You live in Chicago, but you consider Miami home?"

She'd caught him again. For a professional liar, he was telling her the truth an awful lot. "Miami is as close to home as a Cuban should get." He decided to change the subject. "The proper way to drink a Hatuey is to share it with a good friend. We say in Spanish, *'Un indio, dos canoas.'* That means, *'One Indian, two canoes.'* One beer and two glasses."

Rey opened a glass-fronted cabinet. "In that case, here's a canoe for each of us."

He poured the beer, adjusting the foamy head as it climbed the sides of Rey's fine lead-crystal tumblers. "That's the classiest canoe I've ever drunk from."

She smiled as they clinked glasses. "My mother brought them from Ireland as a loft-warming present. I didn't have the heart to tell her I'd prefer new space heaters or an industrial-strength central vacuum."

He sipped his beer, rolling the cool, tangy liquor around his mouth. "The next time I'm in Miami, I'll drink a Hatuey in her honor."

"She'd be pleased. She and my father love trying new beverages, new food and new countries. We traveled the whole world. In fact, I even vacationed in Cuba when I was a kid."

Marco froze, the beer roiling in his stomach. "It's illegal for United States citizens to visit Cuba without permission from the government."

She shrugged. "I wasn't an American citizen until after I went to Cuba, so we traveled on our Swedish passports."

"What did you do in Cuba?" How bizarre it was to talk to her about Cuba, as if it were a fun tropical destination.

"We toured Havana and did some scuba diving on the southern coast." She traced her finger through a puddle of condensation on the countertop.

"Did you dive at *La Isla de la Juventud?*" He clutched the Irish crystal. The so-called Isle of Youth was world renowned for fantastic scuba diving. That and its notorious political prison. His poor *papá.*

She thought for a second. The sharp facets cut into his palm as he waited for her answer. "No, we dove at the Gardens of the Queen. They were the most beautiful reefs I'd ever seen. Teeming with thousands of grouper fish, glittering silver tarpon and even reef sharks. It was so unspoiled."

"Ah, yes. Unspoiled because the only people allowed to visit them are rich foreigners and Cuban bureaucrats." He thunked down his glass.

She stared at him. "Well. I guess it's time to get to work." She set down her own half-full glass of beer and stood.

Mierda. Why couldn't he keep his mouth shut? "No, Rey, I'm sorry." He came around the bar and grabbed her elbow. She spun toward him. He let go, but not before the heavy weight of her breast bumped his hand. He was right. There was nothing between her luscious breasts and the thin blue silk.

"You'll find the robe in the cubicle." Her eyes were the color of a glacier and about as warm.

"Please." The word grated rustily. "I, um, have a sore spot about Cuba. Life there was very difficult for my family after my father died."

She gasped. "I'm so sorry to hear that. How awful for you." Her blue eyes sparkled with sympathetic tears.

"It's okay, really." God, had he lost his touch with a beautiful woman or what? First he pissed her off and then he made her cry. "Why don't you tell me about your family?" He wanted to know something about her beyond her beautiful face and phenomenal body.

She blinked and finally smiled, her lips curving over the tumbler's rim. "My father was appointed as an assistant to the Swedish consulate here. My mother was disappointed we weren't sent to New York or Washington, D.C., but my father told her she was lucky he wasn't posted to Nebraska or Minnesota. They get more snow than Chicago."

"Impossible." Marco had considered heading to Minneapolis once he took care of business in Chicago. The more he kept on the move, the better. On the other hand, he had a relatively secure place to stay, and no one would expect him to take a job modeling nude, of all things.

He looked at the blond beauty across the table from him. Who was he kidding? He just wanted a chance to stop pretending, a chance to stop running. Rey was so warm, so caring, even finding Cuban beer in the middle of Chicago for him.

Marco Flores was tired and chilled to the bone. Maybe it was time for him to come in from the cold, even for just a little while.

8

IT WAS AS IF A CLOUD lifted off Marco's face. Rey relaxed a bit on her stool, glad for the lighter atmosphere. "You were lucky to grow up where it's warm. Swedes catch cabin fever after a dozen feet of snow every winter and no daylight for months."

"People in the tropics are usually easygoing, especially the tourists after a few days of rum and sun." He sipped his Cuban beer. She admired the press of his lips against the crystal, the long brown column of his throat as he swallowed.

He finished his beer and smiled at her. "In Miami you can often see a beautiful blonde walking on the beach, the ocean breeze blowing her gauzy skirts against her thighs."

Rey stared at him, her own gauzy skirt growing damp between her legs.

He continued. "A dark-haired man smiles at her, hoping she'll stop and talk to him."

"Does she?" Rey's throat was dry.

"It depends. If she already has a lover waiting for her at her hotel, she passes by."

"And what if she doesn't have a lover?"

His voice caressed her like the sea breezes he'd described. Instead of being cool and soothing, his words made her hot and flustered. "If she likes his looks, she'll smile back and invite him for a drink."

Rey gulped her beer, welcoming its earthy tang. "She likes his looks. Then what?"

He plucked the glass from her hand and set it on the polished countertop, the flecks of mica matching the golden flecks in his eyes. "He holds her hand and tells her she's the sexiest, most beautiful woman he's ever met." He took her hand and rubbed his thumb over the sensitive skin of her knuckles.

He slid off his stool and strode around to her. "After one or two drinks, he invites her to dance, wanting her body pressed against his."

As he pulled her close, she gasped. He was aroused and not embarrassed to show her. His erection rubbed on the cradle of her thighs. She twined her arms around his neck, running her fingers through the soft curls covering the strong muscles of his neck. The jazz segued into a slow, throbbing beat as they swayed together, separated only by a few thin layers of fabric.

She rubbed her tingling breasts against his chest, joining in his fantasy. "After they dance for a few minutes, she invites him to her hotel room to see the ocean view from her balcony."

His hot gaze dropped to her deep cleavage. "And he gladly accepts, knowing the view inside the room is even better."

He took her hand and started to lead her to the sheet-covered chaise instead of her bedroom. She balked.

"What's wrong?" He caressed her wrist, sending shivers up her spine.

She stared at the wide expanse of pure Egyptian cotton. Despite her dating a few of her models, the chaise had always been for work, not pleasure. How was she supposed to draw Marco tomorrow? "You're the most appealing man I've met in a long time."

"By 'appealing,' do you mean arousing?" His husky voice curled around her, warming her down to her toes.

She caught her breath. "Yes. But if we have sex…"

"When we make love," he corrected her.

"If." She threw him a quelling look. "Look, I've had relationships with a couple of my models. The last one decided to handle our breakup by spreading scummy gossip about me to his model friends."

"Reina." He stepped closer to her. "I would never gossip about you. To ease your worries, I don't know a soul in the Chicago modeling scene."

"Except Susan."

"Who?"

"Susan, your modeling agent."

"Right. My agent." He tucked a strand of her hair behind her ear, stroking the sensitive rim. She leaned into his hand as he continued his caress across her jaw. "And I would never tell her. What we do as a man and woman is nobody's business."

Business. That word brought her back to her initial purpose in inviting him over. If her dislike of Craig had shown in his painting, maybe her passion for Marco would show in his statue. It was what she'd wanted when she thought of her plan. So why did it seem so calculating?

He lifted her hand and kissed the inside of her wrist, just like that Spanish pirate movie. His eyes never left hers. "What do you want, Reina?" His voice was low and seductive.

She took a deep breath. "I want you." Her voice came out strong and clear.

"You'll have me." His eyes were full of promise. "And I'll have you."

His words sent a rush of desire through her middle. She took his other hand in hers and tugged him to the chaise.

He kissed her hard, his lips firm and warm on hers, his tongue teasing the seam of her mouth. His big hands slipped over her bottom, massaging and cupping her buttocks.

She flinched. He stopped. "What is it?" Concern tempered the desire in his eyes.

"Nothing." He'd never understand, having the perfect physique himself.

"Tell me."

"I'm, um, just self-conscious about my butt." Thanks, Mom. Getting gift certificates for liposuction hadn't helped her self-confidence.

He stared at her. "You think your bottom is too big? This luscious ass?" He pushed his hands under the elastic waistband of her skirt and muttered something in Spanish. "*Dios mío,* are you wearing any panties?"

She felt surprisingly shy. "Just a thong."

"Like two halves of a velvety peach." He shoved her skirt to the floor and wiggled his fingers into the dripping folds between her thighs. "Ripe and juicy."

He dropped to his knees in front of her, nuzzling her mound. She clutched his shoulders. "A see-through thong? You didn't want to draw pictures of me at all tonight, did you?" Her knees weakened as his hot mouth scorched her through the ivory mesh.

His finger dipped under the silk thread dividing her buttocks. His throat convulsed.

She shuddered as he moved up her body to drag his tongue along the sensitive tendons in her neck, stopping to lick the racing pulse at the base of her throat. A clean citrus scent rose off his thick black curls.

She reached for the silken knot at her waist, but he stopped her. "Let me." Instead of untying the knot, he ran his fingertips along the exposed V of skin. Her heart thumped so hard she thought it would knock his fingers away.

Unfastening the top button, he spread the fabric open and licked the top slope of each breast. Then the next button, right at the level of her aching nipples.

"No bra." He nuzzled the delicate skin over her breastbone. She squirmed, wanting his mouth on her. "God, I could tell when you bent over to look in the fridge. I thought your nipples were hard from the cold air, but that wasn't it. You've been flashing those little diamond points at me because you're hot for me, aren't you?"

She thought about denying it, but a telltale flush crept up her chest, right where his cheek rested against her. The rumble of his laughter vibrated against her skin.

"A blush? It's been years since I met a woman who can still blush."

"I just have fair skin, that's all." He was right. She didn't blush easily, but Marco lowered the defenses she'd built since Stefan.

"So fair." His tongue laved the full curves peeping from

between her lapels. "Mmm. Like sugar and cream. Sweet and smooth, waiting for my tongue to glide over you."

She clutched his head to her, desperate for him to suck her nipples, pull her deep into his mouth and relieve the pulsing throb darting from them to between her thighs.

He paused before the last button, running his fingertips over her breasts but deliberately avoiding the aching peaks. "*Querida,* I just got a late Christmas gift. A beautifully wrapped package with an even more beautiful gift inside."

His words touched her but also made her uncomfortable. He wasn't supposed to be so sweet and romantic. "I like your package, too," she joked, trying to put them on a lighter footing. She stroked the impressive bulge in the front of his tight black pants.

His breath hitched and he grabbed her hand. "Any more of that and this package won't wait to be opened. I haven't finished unwrapping you." He yanked at the final button and her shirt gaped open.

She made a move to untie the knot at her waist, but he stopped her. "No, leave it." He stood for a heartbeat and pulled the silk taut across her breasts, admiring the effect. "I like the way your nipples jut against the silk."

She gasped as he slipped his hands under the lapels of her open shirt and sucked her silk-covered nipple deep into his mouth.

The wet silk molded itself to her aching skin. He blew on one peak, and it stiffened under the cool stream of air even more.

He moved his mouth to the other side, lavishing the same attention. His heavy body pressed her against the cushioned chaise back. She tugged the waistband of his sweater free, luxuriating in the straight lines of his spine, his well-sculpted trapezius and latissimus dorsi muscles and his hot, smooth skin. But the skin on his cock had been much hotter and smoother.

The naughty thought sent another flood of moisture between her thighs, and she squirmed against his rock-hard abs, the sprinkling of hair on his belly scraping across her pulsing center.

He looked up from her nipples, his eyelids slumberous with desire. "You're burning hot. And so am I." He dragged his sweater over his head. Rey had seen his bare chest twice in person and more times in her fantasies than she cared to admit, but it still made her mouth dry and her knees weak. His warm brown skin stretched tightly over hard pecs and abs. Copper-colored nipples nestled in a mat of black hair that tapered below the black leather belt cinching his narrow waist.

He left his belt fastened despite the huge erection tenting the zipper below. When he bent to touch her, she grabbed his buckle. "I want you inside me."

"Like this?" His finger pushed past her flimsy thong and buried itself deep inside her. "Or like this?" He slipped in a second finger and stroked in and out. She let go of him and fell onto the pillows, her tiny muscles clenching around his strong fingers. He twisted his knuckles as he plunged them deep. Pushing her damp shirt aside, he bared a straining pink peak. He fastened his mouth on her and at the same time circled his thumb over her pulsing knot of nerves. Lightning shot between her nipple and her clitoris, and she bit back a muffled cry.

He lifted his head from her glistening rosy nipple. "I want to hear you scream, *querida*. Scream when I make you come hard."

His fingers quickened, rubbing nerve endings inside her she didn't even know existed. His thumb flicked over her pulsing center, pressing harder and harder with each pass. She thrust her hips against his hand as his teeth nipped the aching tips of her breasts. Her throat grew sore from her increasingly loud cries, but she didn't care. He made magic with his fingers and mouth. Tension spiraled underneath his thumb, and he pinched her other nipple hard. The tension split wide open, exploding and radiating from her center to her breasts and throughout her entire body. Her breath rasped as she screamed his name. She hadn't felt so good in years, if ever. She finally opened her eyes to see his burning gaze.

He hadn't even made it onto the chaise the whole way and was still kneeling on the sealed concrete floor. "I'm glad you enjoyed that." He leaned forward to press a tender kiss on her mouth.

"It's your turn now." She fumbled his pants open, his cock bulging through the zipper. She freed him with trembling hands. He was hot steel filling her hands, long and brown. She stroked him, reveling in the hot, silky skin covering firm, solid flesh. He threw his head back, the tendons in his neck standing out in sharp relief.

"I was right." His heavy balls overflowed her palm. She massaged them as her other hand pumped him gently.

He groaned and jerked, a drop of pearlescent fluid covering his fleshy head. "Right? About what?"

"Your skin is even softer here." She shifted her body. "And now I want to know if you taste as good as you look."

"Oh, God, Reina." He grabbed her upper arms. "If you put your mouth on me, it's all over." He fumbled in his pocket and dragged out a foil packet. "Put this on me and I'll make you scream again."

She unwrapped the condom with shaky hands and slid it onto his thick shaft. His Adam's apple bobbed, his self-control balancing on a knife's edge. As soon as he was protected, he lifted her onto the chaise. She leaned on her elbows, her legs dangling over the edge.

"Lie down. I have an idea."

She complied reluctantly, off balance physically and emotionally. She adjusted her bottom to keep from falling, although if she did, she had plenty of padding to cushion her tailbone.

He lifted her ankle and stroked upward. He darted his tongue into the sensitive hollow behind her knee and she jumped. "You taste great here. Makes me wonder how you taste all over."

Her breath caught in her throat. "Marco." Her voice was bedroom-husky and sensual, not sounding like herself at all.

"Not now. I'll find out later." He put her ankle onto his shoulder. She teetered on the edge of the chaise, her thong the only thing that kept her from feeling horribly exposed.

He must have read her mind because he hooked a finger under her waistband. "You won't need this."

She bit back a protest. She did too need her thong, especially after he tossed it on the chaise and ducked his shoulder under her other leg.

Her legs bracketed his head, leaving her wide open and vulnerable. He moved closer, lifting her bottom until only her shoulders rested on the pillows. She twisted slightly, but he brushed his hot mouth along her calf until she relaxed.

He slid his hands up her legs, cupping her bottom in both hands. "God, I am tempted to lick you right here." He parted the folds of her sex gently, and she gasped as he brushed his thumb across her still-throbbing clitoris. He increased the tempo of his caresses, and she lifted her hips even higher into the welcome pressure. A flush of heat pulsed through her body, the rasp of silk over her taut nipples almost unbearable.

If she couldn't get relief from the tension, she would go crazy, and she told him so.

"You want me inside you?" He was as aroused as she was, beads of sweat matting his black chest hair into ringlets.

"Yes!"

He thrust into her.

It was glorious.

His molten gold eyes captured hers when she gasped. "Too deep?" He withdrew a few inches.

"No. More." She shook her head frantically, unable to move her body farther onto his shaft.

"You can have all of me." His shoulders flexed under her calves as he slid back.

She had never been so thoroughly filled. His swollen penis pulsed inside her, stretching her vagina until she cried out from the exquisite pressure.

He cupped and squeezed her buttocks. "You have a great ass. Next time I want to bend you over the chaise and take you from behind." He angled his hips so his head nudged the entrance to her womb, withdrawing and thrusting. She bowed her body to accommodate the deep penetration. She wasn't afraid of losing her balance anymore because he was rock-steady around her and inside her.

"You're so wet and tight around me. I can tell you want to come so bad." He was on the edge, too, a sheen of sweat gilding his skin despite the cool air. He reached between their bodies and stroked her clit.

She moaned and twisted in his intimate embrace, wanting release from his finger slipping over her and his cock slipping inside her. His slow, relentless pace forced her to hang over a delirious precipice until her hold broke and she tumbled, pulling him with her as his control shattered and he fell into her eager body, moaning long, liquid gushes of Spanish endearments.

Marco sprawled on his stomach as if he hadn't slept in days, his body solid and heavy.

Rey crept from under his arm and pulled on the midnight-blue terry-cloth robe draped over a nearby chair. She found her art supplies and dragged her stool close to him.

For the first time in weeks she drew for the sheer pleasure of it, scratching the charcoal feverishly over the pristine white pages of her sketch pad. Finally here was her Roman god, the black spirals of his hair, the long sculpted lines of his scarred back, the curves of his thick palms and the high arches of his feet.

She flipped her pad over to a fresh page, intent on sketching his face in detail. His eyes opened slowly. Her stomach fluttered at his lazy golden gaze as he rolled over onto his side.

"You're going to hurt my feelings. I thought I'd tired you enough that we wouldn't work tonight. Come here." He patted the sheet exactly as Craig, her last nude model, had.

This time she tossed aside her sketch pad and dropped the robe. When a Roman god issued a command to join him in bed, what mortal woman could resist?

MARCO PEERED THROUGH THE curtains at his brother's apartment. He'd been extremely cautious after almost strangling the homeless guy near Rey's loft.

Francisco's audition had gone well and he was preparing for a screen test. Marco hadn't heard from his *mamá,* so no news was good news.

He pulled out the cell phone he'd bought along with the pistol. He'd rethought his plan of cutting off total contact with any of his DEA buddies and had decided to call his closest friend, Eddie Jones. Eddie was a former college football player from Texas and spoke Spanish as if he were born in Mexico City. He'd brought down several drug runners along the Río Grande and had been a great help to Marco. Now Marco was counting on him even more.

The gun dealer had assured him that the cloned phone, like the pistol, was untraceable. Marco obviously never trusted anyone who sold illegal goods, but he had made it clear that he would be back, pistol in hand, if he encountered any difficulties.

The man had believed him.

Marco sighed. He would be happy to see the last of the cold, intimidating side of his personality, but it had been part of him since he was twelve. Not for the first time Marco considered his future—if he had one. Working undercover for DEA did not accentuate his good qualities, and he was damn sure he didn't want to ride a desk.

Marco pressed the code to block the caller ID and dialed Eddie's private cell number.

"Jones here."

"*Hola,* Lalo." As far as he knew, Marco was the only one who called him Lalo, the common Spanish nickname for Eduardo. Everyone else called him Eddie or Jonesey.

Marco heard a sharp intake of breath and then his friend's slow drawl came over the phone. "Hey, how's it goin'?"

"Still here."

"Uh-huh." Eddie spoke to whoever was with him. "Darlin', I'm gonna step outside for a quick smoke."

"Did I interrupt something?" Marco couldn't resist needling his friend.

"Cut the shit and tell me what the hell's going on! The boss thought you'd already been fed to either the sharks or the gators."

"Someone's rotten in our office. There were only a few people who knew about my informant."

"Yeah, about him…" Eddie cleared his throat. "Metro-Dade PD found enough parts of him to make an ID."

Marco pinched the bridge of his nose and swore a long stream of obscenities.

"Sorry, man. I had a snitch get offed in Mexico once. Guy was no prince but still didn't deserve it."

"Damn it!" Marco had known deep down his snitch

was dead, but hearing the confirmation just made him madder.

"Listen, *mano,* I don't even want to know where you are. We still have Rodríguez under surveillance, but that doesn't mean jack." A cigarette lighter clicked and Eddie sucked in a lungful of smoke.

"I'm safe for now. Nose around at the office and see what you can dig up, but be careful, for God's sake." Marco didn't want to pull Eddie deeper into the mess.

His friend exhaled a long stream of smoke. "Will do. Call me when you can and stay safe, *amigo.*"

"*Hasta la vista,* Eddie."

"You better believe I'll see you later. None of that goodbye shit. Oops, gotta go, my date's coming."

"Is she a screamer or a moaner?"

Eddie told him where to stick it and hung up.

Marco turned off the phone. He'd keep it for a while, since buying another stolen phone would be risky. Especially since he didn't want to get caught with a pistol in his pocket.

Getting arrested for carrying a concealed, illegal weapon would be a real kick to the *cojones.* Jail was full of men willing to kill him for a dime bag of cocaine while the cops worked out who he was.

If it came down to that, what was he willing to do to keep his freedom? Shoot a fellow officer in the shoulder or leg?

Normally he'd rather get shot himself than do that, but his sense of self-preservation had been honed to a razor's edge. He just didn't know what kind of man Marco Flores was anymore.

9

MARCO LET OUT A GUTTURAL cry that mingled with Rey's moans. "Oh, my God, Marco, you're going to kill me." She let go of his shoulders and grimaced as she lowered her wobbly legs from his waist.

"What a headline." He rolled off her and they lay side by side. "'Famous Chicago Artist Comes to Death After a Week of Fantastic Multiple Orgasms.'" It had been a fantastic week for him, too. Over the past year his sexual encounters had been impersonal and furtive, more for physical release than emotional closeness. Celibacy was not an admired trait among Rodríguez's men.

His stomach growled and she giggled, running her fingers over his abs. "'Sexy Model Starves Because He'd Rather Make Love Than Eat.'"

"You think that's funny?" He grabbed her around the waist and tickled her. And if he got to fondle her breasts while she squirmed in his arms, so much the better.

"Stop, stop," she panted among a fit of giggles. "All right, I'll feed you."

"Yum." He rolled on top of her and nibbled on her ear. "What would you like me to eat first?"

"No, I mean real food." She shoved at his chest, her surprisingly strong arms lifting him off her.

He flopped over, throwing his forearm over his head. "I'll take a *café con leche* with some fresh Cuban bread."

Rey sat up, finger-combing the tangles from her hair. "How about Swedish coffee with fresh apple strudel? I know a great bakery not far from here."

He thought fast. He didn't like going out in full daylight, but he'd bundle up and only leave his nose exposed. His stomach gurgled again. "You've got a deal."

She stood and ambled across her bedroom, her shapely ass swaying. He leaped up to follow her and a rush of cold air shriveled his private parts. He put his hands on her butt, enjoying her squeal as he hustled her into the bathroom. "I hope you've got plenty of hot water to warm us."

Giving him a saucy grin, she twisted the chrome faucet in her large tiled shower. "I've got a better idea to warm you."

He grinned and followed her into the stream of water. Winter in Chicago had its benefits after all.

"I'M SO FULL." REY LEANED back and moaned with pleasure.

"Take some more," he coaxed.

"It's too big and thick. Why don't you finish?"

"If you insist." He lifted the éclair and licked a smear of chocolate off his firm upper lip. Rey's stomach quivered with feelings that had nothing to do with overconsumption of French pastry.

Marco noticed her staring at his mouth and set the éclair on the marble-topped café table. Rey had wanted to sit next to the sunny window, but he had tugged her to a table near the kitchen. "Now that we've stoked up on fuel, why don't we go back to your place and burn some of it off?" He was still wearing his sunglasses and brown knit watch cap.

It was a tempting suggestion, especially when he reached over and caressed her hand. But it was a beautiful bright day, and she was still too much of a Swede not to take advantage of any winter sunshine. "Let's take a walk in the beautiful weather."

"Beautiful weather?" He looked out the picture window. "I see six-foot drifts of snow in the corner of the parking lot."

"It's only a couple degrees below freezing. The sunlight is good for you." She pushed back her black wrought-iron chair and reached for her coat. She stroked his smooth jaw, inhaling the fresh scent of his shaving cream. "I told my friend at the Swedish-American Museum I'd stop in if I was in the neighborhood. It's only a few blocks."

His lips tightened and he looked as though he wanted to refuse.

"Please? We won't stay very long, and the cultural center really is a neat little place."

"All right." He took her jacket and held it for her. As she drew it around her shoulders, he wrapped his arms around her from behind. "If I get too cold, will you warm me up?"

He held the bakery door open for her and they strolled outside. The weak sunlight flashed off puddles of salty slush on the uneven sidewalk.

"What is this neighborhood called anyway?" He tucked her hand into his roomy pocket. Even through their gloves his heat warmed her.

"Andersonville, after the Swedish immigrants who came here in the 1800s."

"It seems to have changed a bit." He glanced at an Armenian restaurant, several trendy bistros and a bakery for dogs.

"Only on the surface. It still has the immigrant attitude that anything is possible, that you can leave your old life behind and create something new and wonderful."

"Like you've done with your artwork."

"Yes, I suppose." Irrational discontent pricked at her. Her initial sketches of Marco were fabulous, her agent was thrilled and she'd had more orgasms in the last week than in her entire life. She'd told Marco about her family and friends, but he still held back any personal information. "So what kind of new life did you create for yourself?"

He laughed. "I was just a kid. The only life I created was what my mother wanted. Go to school, stay out of trouble and don't embarrass the family."

"Well, now that you're an adult, you don't have to listen to your mother."

"Not listen to my mother? You've never met a Cuban *mamá*, have you? Or worse yet, a Cuban *abuelita?* That's Spanish for grandmother, by the way."

"No, I never have."

He shivered in mock terror. "Those ladies are scary. I've seen hardened criminals on their knees, pleading. 'Oh, please don't let my mother post bail. I'd rather go to jail than go home and have her smack me with her cane.' Pathetic." He shook his head.

"And where did you run into hardened criminals?"

His fingers tightened infinitesimally over hers and deliberately relaxed. "A misspent youth."

"Really?" Rey flicked a glance at his profile, realizing that he hadn't answered her question about what kind of life he'd made for himself after leaving Cuba.

"I fell in with the wrong crowd, goofed off in school and chased too many girls. Of course, none of them was as beautiful as you." He swept her into his arms, his lips warming hers in the cold Chicago sunlight until she forgot what she'd wanted to ask him.

10

MARCO WATCHED THE OTHER pedestrians, his mirrored sunglasses concealing the direction of his gaze. None was an obvious candidate to be on Rodríguez's payroll, especially not the East Indian woman berating her dawdling teenage son window-shopping the latest PlayStation releases. He smiled to himself. Mothers sounded alike in any language.

Rey saw the duo and laughed. Still holding his hand, she turned slightly as they walked to the museum. "What did your mother do when you fell into bad company? She couldn't have been old enough to whack you with her cane."

He didn't want to answer any more personal questions because it was getting harder and harder to lie to her. "Nothing so drastic. She grounded me from watching my favorite TV shows."

"Yeah, that's what my mother always tried. Until she realized I'd rather paint. So she grounded me from my art supplies instead." She grinned at him. "What was your favorite TV show?"

He sighed, a long stream of air spiraling in front of him like dragon's breath. *"Miami Vice."*

"A hometown show. Cool."

"Pretty exciting stuff," he agreed. But the eighties cop show had meant more to him than fast cars, scantily clad women and beating up bad guys. If his buddies at DEA ever found out Sonny Crockett and Ricardo Tubbs were his inspiration to go into law enforcement, their howls of laughter would be heard from Miami to Jacksonville. They'd probably buy him a white linen blazer and pink shirt just for kicks.

She shook her head. "Moms always know just how to drive you crazy. Mine sure does. At least she and my father are out of the country and not around to pester me."

"Yeah, my mother's traveling now, too. She recently got married to an old friend of the family and they're on a honeymoon cruise."

"Your mother's on her honeymoon? That's so sweet."

"Sweet?" Marco made a sour face. "I guess. At least Luis is a decent guy. Their cruise ship is touring the Mediterranean for at least six weeks." Long enough to keep his mother safe until Marco's testimony in February.

"Six weeks? That's a long cruise."

He'd paid for it over their objections as a wedding gift, but it was worth it. "The ship will visit Spain, the south of France, Italy and the Greek isles."

"Wow." She was impressed. "A honeymoon fit for a queen."

"She deserves it. She's been alone for a long time." To his shock, his throat clogged. Dammit. It had been over twenty years, but he still missed his father.

"What a lucky woman." Her blue eyes were suspiciously bright. "Not only to find love a second time but to have a wonderful son like you." She squeezed his gloved hand.

His cheeks reddened and he tried to tell himself it was windburn. Fortunately for his Cuban sense of machismo, they arrived at the Swedish museum and he was spared from more undeserved praise.

"Oh, look, we're here." He stopped in front of the wide set of polished granite steps. "Shall we go in?"

Rey gave him a fishy look but didn't press him. She ran lightly up the stairs, her boots crunching on the chunks of rock salt used to melt ice. She was obviously eager to see her friend.

He stopped midstep. Was her friend an old boyfriend? She'd said she wasn't seeing anybody, but a woman as beautiful and intelligent as Rey was sure to have a few exes. He followed her grimly, imagining a six-and-a-half-foot-tall Viking named Sven with golden hair and sky-blue eyes. He had a sudden hatred for guys like that.

She waited for him at the top of the steps and he opened the heavy glass door for her. She thanked him and walked in, pulling off her gloves and cute little fleecy hat. She unzipped her parka, her full breasts outlined under her snug blue fluffy sweater.

Growing up in Miami, he'd seen his share of breasts, some covered by the legal minimum, some not. But there was something naughty about breasts under a nice tight sweater that invited a man to strip it off and see for himself.

"Look, she's here!" Rey ran across the lobby, her hiking boots squeaking on the wet floor.

She? He tamped down the rush of relief and followed her.

"Freya! How are you?" An elegant ash-blond woman in her fifties came from behind the reception desk and greeted Rey with a kiss on each cheek.

"Annike, I hoped you'd be volunteering today. It's been so long since we've seen each other." Marco was amused to hear Rey's Swedish accent deepen to match her friend's.

"Too long, dear." Rey and her friend started chatting in Swedish. Marco contented himself with listening to their singsong voices. Rey's youthful beauty along with Annike's mature good looks was a happy combination for any man to watch. If Annike were any example of how Swedish women aged, Rey would still be beautiful in thirty years.

The man who loved her in thirty years would be lucky. Envy for that unknown man jabbed into him, unexpected and unwelcome. Why should he care? He couldn't stay around for thirty days, much less thirty years. Men like him never could. He had gone into the DEA knowing it would be like this, and considering a long-term relationship was sheer foolishness. No matter how he might wish otherwise.

Rey caught him watching her and abruptly switched into English. "I'm sorry, Marco. Annike, this is my friend Marco Flores. Marco, this is my first art teacher and dear friend, Annike Peterson. She started me on my art career."

"Oh, Rey." Annike gave her young friend a fond look. "You give me too much credit. You would have discovered your artistic talent the first time you picked up a brush."

"No, no." Rey hugged her. "But I have an exhibition in February. You have to come."

"I wouldn't miss it," Annike promised. "The museum is hosting a social evening for singles next month, but it doesn't look like you'd be interested." Her knowing smile was a punch in the gut. Next month he'd be in Miami and Rey would be free to meet tall, blond men at Swedish singles' night.

"No, not this time," Rey replied lightly. "Today we're just here for a quick visit."

Just then a troop of Scouts jostled into the museum. "Ah, here's my two-o'clock tour." She extended her hand to Marco and he shook it gently. "It was a pleasure to meet you, Marco." She muttered something in Swedish and turned to greet the troop leaders.

Rey leaned into Marco. "Annike was praying for help."

"You'd think the Swedish-American Museum would be used to Viking raiders."

"Not the eight-year-old variety."

"That's true. Those horned helmets would fall over their eyes."

"That's just a Hollywood myth." She grabbed his elbow and a jolt of desire shot up his arm. He looked at her smiling face and let her drag him down the corridor.

"I thought since you were an immigrant, too, you might like the immigration exhibit."

"*Querida,* anyone who comes from Cuba is a refugee, plain and simple."

"Refugee or no, it's designed to show children the immigrant experience," she said. "Of course, I came to America on an SAS flight from Stockholm."

It was just another reason not to get attached to her. Even their immigration experiences were worlds apart. "What does the exhibit have, a replica of the waiting room at Immigration and Naturalization Services?"

"It's a bit more interesting than that." She turned the corner. He almost bumped into her because he'd been admiring the wiggle of her hips.

"Isn't that great?" She pointed to the exhibit.

Great. A boat.

He'd come a millimeter away from dying only twice in his life. Both times it had been on a boat.

Rey ran up the gangplank. "Come on, Marco. Let's play on the ship."

"Rey, this is a kid's exhibit. I don't want to break it."

"Don't be silly. We're the only ones here. It'll be fun."

At least it didn't look like the raft he'd ridden in from Cuba. It wasn't sinking. Or like the yacht he'd dived off when his cover was blown. Nobody was shooting at him.

He stepped on the deck, the wood creaking. Rey ran to the front, her steps shaking the planks under his boots. "Can you imagine it, Marco?"

He didn't have to.

"A tiny ship bobbing in the vast Atlantic Ocean. No sonar, no cell phones, no way to call for help if disaster threatened. Twenty-foot-high waves tossing the fragile vessel back and forth, up and down, side to side." Rey swayed, riding the stormy seas.

Marco sighed. The reality was much less romantic. Pissing over the side of the raft, lips cracking from dehydration, skin burning from the sun's rays bouncing off the ocean.

"The only protection from brutal storms and waves was a thin wooden hull."

"Uh-huh."

"Marco, if you're bored, just tell me. We can look at many more exhibits here in the museum. Or we can leave."

Oh, no. He'd hurt her feelings. He actually liked boats, often borrowing his buddy's to go deep-sea fishing. And after all, he was from Miami, the boating capital of the universe.

"Okay, let's go." Rey passed him and he caught her elbow.

He opened his mouth to say something noncommittal and soothing. Instead he blurted out everything. "We came from Cuba on a raft not much bigger than this." He didn't know why he'd let that slip. He never discussed how he'd left Cuba.

She stopped and stared at him. "You took a raft across the ocean?"

"Yeah, we had a rough crossing and took on lots of water." Now that he'd told her, the story flooded out of him. "My baby brother got hurt, and there were sharks circling us." Both marine and human. "My mother counted on me. I was the man of the family, but I couldn't protect them."

"Protect them? From what?"

"Weather, waves and lots of criminals leaving Cuba at the same time." He didn't want to say more.

"Marco, you weren't more than a child yourself. Did your family make it safely?"

"More or less."

"Then you did your job. I'm sure your mother was glad for your help."

He was touched at her thoughtfulness. He cupped her jaw. "I'm glad you showed me this boat."

The funny thing was, he *was* glad. He pulled Rey close for a hug. Wrapping his arms around her, he nuzzled her neck.

She snuggled close. "When we met, you reminded me of a Spanish pirate in an old Saturday-afternoon movie."

Marco smiled into her floral-scented hair. She was closer to the truth than she thought. He'd raided several ships in his line of work. "Not a Spanish pirate. They lisp, throwing in *th*s all over the place. How about a Cuban pirate? They find the best booty." His hand cupped her ass. She pulled away, but slowly, so he got a firm squeeze in.

"Behave yourself. This is a children's museum." She tipped her head and smiled. "But you have the look— dark, handsome and more than a bit dangerous. A perfect swashbuckler."

"Ahoy, wench, want to unbuckle my swash?" He grabbed her hand and slid it to the bulge beneath his slim silver belt buckle.

"Marco!" Rey yanked her hand away and waggled a finger under his nose. "This is not the place."

He grabbed her hand again and guided it back. "Oh, yes, *this* is the place."

"You know what I mean," she sputtered. The scouts burst in the door and stampeded to the wooden boat exhibit. She gave him a see-I-told-you-so look.

He guided Rey off the boat. "What would you like to show me now?" He purposely deepened his voice and leered at her.

They walked hand in hand around the corner. She pointed to a closed door. "That's the art classroom. Annike still teaches painting classes like the one I took."

"How old were you when you began painting?" He figured eighteen was the minimum legal age for drawing naked men.

"I was twelve."

"Twelve?" Marco had heard Scandinavians were very comfortable with nudity, but hey, come on. "And your parents were okay with that?"

"Well, it was just a hobby at first, but when I attended more and more classes, they realized I had a serious interest."

At twelve he'd had a serious interest in naked women, but he didn't think his *mamá* would have let him go to art class to paint them.

"I had trouble getting the fine details right at first, like getting the right shade of pink and making sure all the veins went in the right direction, but Annike is an expert."

"She is?" Marco's mind boggled at the image of the elegant Annike kneeling to examine some male model's penis.

"Oh, yes. She started painting when she was a young girl in Sweden. This kind of painting has a long and respected tradition in Scandinavia."

Marco couldn't keep silent anymore. "What kind of parents let you paint naked men when you were only twelve?"

"Paint naked men when I was twelve?" Rey stopped dead and stared at him. "What are you talking about?"

"Getting the right shade of pink and making sure the veins ran in the right direction. I think you're a great artist, but I don't think it's proper for young girls to paint pictures of naked men."

Rey looked puzzled. "I agree." Understanding dawned on her face. "Oh, Marco. You thought Annike painted naked men?" She bent at the waist and laughed until her ivory cheeks turned red.

"My Cuban upbringing might be more conservative than your Swedish background, but…" He stopped as Rey waved her hand. Straightening and stifling a couple more giggles, she cupped his jaw with her long fingers.

"You are a *good* man, Marco Flores." She stood on tiptoe and pressed a brief kiss on his mouth. He savored the spicy cinnamon taste of her lips. She pulled away after a minute and smiled at him. "Annike doesn't teach nude painting here at the Swedish-American Museum. She teaches traditional Swedish decorative painting."

"No naked men?" Marco felt a mixture of relief and embarrassment.

"Nope. We painted floral designs on chairs, tables, small wooden plaques. I always had trouble mixing the right shade of pink for the flowers and making sure the veins on the leaves went in the right direction." She smiled at him and laced her fingers through his, his hand wrapping around hers. "I didn't draw nude men until I was eighteen and in art school. Men are much more interesting than flowers."

"I'm glad you think so. If you'd become a florist, we might not have met." He pulled her into the shadows of a darkened exhibit. "Let's go in here."

Rey looked at the display. It was new since she'd last visited the museum. Life-size replicas of Viking bards told their epic stories around a bonfire under a midnight-blue ceiling twinkling with tiny fiber-optic stars. "That redheaded Viking looks like my uncle Lars."

He moved behind her as she gazed at the hairy, bearded figures. "That's nice," he said, cupping her shoulders. He wasn't paying attention to the exhibit at all. "Tell me about the first time you drew a naked man."

His intimate tone made her breath catch. "Why?"

"When I model, I want to make sure I'm doing it right."

"You're doing just fine." Her voice wasn't as steady as she'd hoped.

"What did that model do?"

"If it helps you…"

"It will. I like to know how you like it. So I can do it for you."

Oh, he did it for her just fine. She dragged herself back to that time ten years ago when she'd realized the power and beauty of the male body. "He lay on a sheet-draped chaise longue."

"Like the one in your studio."

The chaise where he'd put her ankles on his shoulders and thrust into her. "Yes." She had to clear her throat.

"Then what did you do?"

"At first I concentrated on sketching the lines and curves of his arms and legs. I was too embarrassed to focus on anything else. I was very young and inexperienced."

"Inexperienced with naked men?"

"Totally." She'd been a virgin, in fact.

"And then?"

"The scratch of charcoal on rough-toothed drawing paper was the only sound in the room. I left his face and genitals for last. When I finally drew his face, I could tell he was bored, but he didn't move." Rey's breath quickened. The quiet darkness wrapped them in a sensual blanket.

"Our eyes met. Suddenly, he was more than just a collection of curved lines and shadows. The essence of his spirit leapt out at me."

"Mmm." Marco hummed deep in his throat, sending vibrations down her back. His strong chest and arms sheltered her in warmth.

"When I looked, *really* looked, at what I'd drawn, it was crap. Charcoal scribbles without meaning, without anything. I tore the paper off my sketch pad and threw it on the floor.

"I hardly had to look at the fresh paper as I drew. My charcoal stick knew where to go. The model couldn't look away from me. His gray eyes darkened to black and his breathing quickened."

"Did it make you hot to watch him lie there naked?"

"Yes," Rey whispered. "I focused on drawing the thick, long lines of his penis." Marco's own penis thickened and lengthened against her bottom. She could hardly believe she was getting so aroused in a public place.

Marco had to touch her silky skin before he went crazy. He slipped his hand underneath her soft, fluffy sweater and thin turtleneck, caressing the bare skin of her belly. His finger dipped under her waistband, brushing the top edge of her bikini panties. "What happened next?" he whispered.

"My mouth was suddenly dry, so I licked my lips and his eyes narrowed." She shifted against his crotch, rubbing her curvy little ass across his throbbing cock.

"He got hard." Her voice was breathy as he cupped her breast, her nipple springing to life under his stroking finger.

"Who could blame him? He was probably imagining your little pink tongue licking across his cock." He swooped in and circled his own tongue around the perfect shell of her ear.

She shuddered. "The instructor ended the session right away."

"Why?" he asked absentmindedly, pinching her nipple.

"You know why." Her voice was teasing. "Erections in an art class are a big no-no."

"Really?"

"Of course." She turned in his arms. "Haven't you come across that rule? If a model keeps getting aroused in front of a class, the instructor may not hire him to pose anymore."

"Oh. Right." He'd made another goof by not knowing anything about the modeling scene. He tried to return to their cocoon of sensuality. "I remember being very aroused by you the first time we met. Why did you hire me?"

Even in the dim light he saw her cheeks flush. "In a one-on-one modeling situation, it's up to the artist's discretion what's acceptable."

"Was I acceptable?" He swiveled his hips into hers, his erection settling into the welcoming juncture of her thighs.

She inhaled sharply. "Very acceptable. But we're on the brink of being unacceptable here."

He heard the Scouts approaching again and knew their privacy would be shattered in a few seconds. He whispered in her ear, "Let's go to the loft. I can do some more modeling for you."

"Oh." She looked disappointed.

He bit her earlobe, rasping his tongue and teeth along the soft flesh. "Modeling how I lick your nipples, modeling how I grab your lush, curvy ass, modeling how I slide my cock deep inside you until you scream."

She shuddered in his arms, almost coming from his words. "If we hurry, we can catch the next bus."

He grinned. "Forget public transportation. I'll spring for a taxi."

MARCO SLAMMED THE LOFT door shut and pushed Rey against it. "You're in trouble now, lusty wench." He nipped her neck, grinding his body into hers.

She broke into a fit of giggles. "What? I didn't do anything."

"What do you call unzipping my pants in the taxi and wrapping those long fingers around my cock?" He couldn't believe she'd done that. The fifteen-minute cab ride had been torture. Only the cabbie's watchful eye and a residual regard for public decency had kept him from grabbing her wrist and pumping her hand up and down.

"Did you want my mouth on you instead?" Damned if she didn't circle her pouty lips with her clever pink tongue.

He groaned and yanked open her parka.

"I know exactly what you need." She started toward her bedroom. "Come get undressed."

"I plan to." He grabbed her lush hips and cradled them against his rock-hard penis.

Flushed, she wiggled against him for a second before slipping away. "I have a treat for you." She walked past her bedroom and opened what he'd thought was a closet door. Instead a small wooden hut with a glass door nestled in an alcove. Rey flipped a switch and the hut lit up. Pale wooden benches lined the matching wood-paneled walls. Rey opened the door and stepped in.

"Is that what I think it is?" Marco stood in the hut's open doorway.

"It's my very own personal sauna. I bought it with my first commission check. The heater is top-of-the-line." Rey smiled as she turned knobs on the side of an upright stainless-steel box. "You've had a sauna before, haven't you?"

"Miami is one huge sauna, but yes, I used to go to the steam room at the health club." The heater began to hum, and so did Marco's sense of anticipation. There was plenty of room on the benches for two, especially if those two were sitting extremely close together. Or one inside the other.

Rey carried a hammered-copper bucket with a wooden handle out of the sauna and filled it at the nearby faucet. "The steam and heat will help you warm up. It should be ready in a few minutes." She pulled a fluffy white towel from the cabinet and hung it on the rack next to her own pink satin bathrobe. He imagined the satin slipping over Rey's generous curves, clinging to her full breasts, outlining their firm tips. It was definitely time to get steamy, sauna or no.

He yanked his sweater over his head and unbuttoned the collar of his long-sleeved thermal T-shirt. After that he still had a thin T-shirt underneath. *Dios mío,* it was hard to get naked in this city.

He emerged bare-chested from his pile of winter clothes. Rey wasn't getting naked at all. What was the deal?

"When you go in, sit on the towel and use this ladle to throw water on the rocks to create steam." She set the full bucket inside the sauna.

"Isn't this sauna big enough for two?"

She blinked as if she'd never considered it. "I suppose. I've never used the sauna with anyone else."

He was glad to hear it. They could lose their sauna virginity together. "Come into the sauna with me."

She caught her lush bottom lip between her teeth. "In Scandinavia men and women don't use the sauna together."

"They don't?" What a waste of naked skin and steam.

She shook her head. "The sauna is traditionally a nonsexual activity. Sometimes family members share a sauna, but that's all."

"I'd really be more comfortable if you were there with me." He put what he hoped was a winning smile on his face.

"Well…" She tipped her head to the side, considering his request.

"If I faint from the heat, you can drag me out by the ankles." As if someone who grew up in Cuba without air-conditioning wasn't used to heat and humidity.

"All right. Just for a few minutes until you acclimatize yourself." She pulled another towel from the cabinet.

"Great." He unbuckled his belt and pushed his jeans and briefs to the floor and kicked them aside. "I'm the only one naked. You have to catch up, beautiful."

Her breasts rose and fell rapidly and her pink tongue peeped out to moisten her lips, the towel dropping from her suddenly loose grip. She broke eye contact and stooped to grab it, her pale hair falling in a curtain across her pink cheeks.

Tenderness crept over him for this woman who dealt

with naked men all day but still blushed when he complimented her.

She stood and draped her towel next to his, smoothing the terry cloth until it hung in perfect pleats. She was fussing with the other towel when he crossed the small space to stand behind her. He stopped, his palms sweaty. He hadn't been so nervous since his last undercover mission. He was too damn eager for her and he didn't like it. If she were naked and writhing under him, he could drive away the strange longing in his blood.

"Are you hot, Reina?" he whispered in her ear. She stood as still as one of her statues, gripping the towel.

"The sauna is almost ready." Her voice was a husky whisper.

"I can't wait to take a sauna with you. Watching the hot, steamy air touching every inch of your naked body. Making you wet and dripping." His hand glided between her denim-clad thighs. "Do you like being hot and wet?"

She let out a low, sexy moan and shifted her legs wider. He stroked her center, its heat and moisture radiating through her jeans.

"Let's start with this sweater." He slipped his hands inside her heavy sweater, cupping a breast in each palm. "Such a shame to cover these." He pulled her sweater off and ran his fingers over her nipples.

Static electricity from the sky-blue wool drew her golden goddess hair into an angelic halo. Some strands clung to his face, and he inhaled the clean floral scent of her shampoo. "I love the way you smell."

She patted her flyaway hair. Even through her thick turtleneck her nipples elongated and stiffened. He brushed his thumbs over the tight nubs, pinching them gently.

She sighed and rolled her head to the side. He tried to slide his tongue along the side of her neck but only managed to lick her high collar. A piece of lint stuck to his tongue. He tried to scrape it off with his teeth, but the damn thread wouldn't budge. He let go of one of her breasts.

Rey murmured in protest and turned her head. When she saw him picking the fluffy fiber out of his mouth, she laughed.

"Enough of these damn clothes. I want you naked, Reina." He lunged for her, but she took a step back.

"No touching allowed if you want me to take a sauna with you," she commanded, a teasing glint in her eye. "Sit on the bench out here until I'm ready for you."

He looked at her flushed cheeks and jutting nipples. "I think you're ready for me."

"Marco…" She stood with her hands on her hips until he obeyed, reluctantly sitting next to the copper bucket. He shivered at the cool, smooth wood against his overheated testicles.

Rey stepped away from him and gripped the bottom of her turtleneck and raised it. His breathing accelerated and he caught a glimpse of skin above her waist. As she inched up the shirt, the undersides of her breasts appeared. He bit his knuckle. She was wearing sheer black lace.

Slowly Rey revealed the full curves of her breasts. The bra's demicups barely contained her bounty, the rosy rims of her nipples peeking out from the top. He wanted to suck on them until she screamed his name. She pulled the shirt over her head and dropped it to the floor.

"Much better." She stretched her arms over her head, and her nipples popped free of the lace cups. "Oh, my goodness." She looked at them in mock surprise.

"Do you like my bra?" She cupped her breasts.

"Yes." It came out as a croak.

"It seems a bit small." She brushed the pink tips of her nipples, caught above the cups. "Of course, my nipples aren't usually so hard and pointy. Do you think that might be the problem?"

"I don't." He paused and cleared his throat. "I don't think that's a problem."

She reached for the front clasp and flicked it open. Her heavy breasts spilled into her hands. "Much better." She lifted and squeezed them, massaging the soft white flesh.

His testicles tightened, and a drop of fluid oozed onto the tip of his cock. Any more and he'd make a mess on the floor. "I thought you said no touching allowed."

"I never said I couldn't touch myself." She released her breasts and unbuttoned her jeans. She eased the zipper open until Marco saw a tiny triangle of black lace peeping through the opening.

He caught a glimpse of the blond curls between her legs pressed against the lace. "Do you like to touch yourself, Reina?" If she said yes, he would have to empty the copper bucket over his lap to keep from exploding.

She gave him a sultry smile as she pushed down her jeans until they puddled around her ankles. "Sometimes." She turned slightly and he nearly swallowed his tongue.

The miniature scrap of lace couldn't hide the engorged lips of her sex, the swollen nub pulsing. The thong's narrow band dipped between the full curves of her bottom, framing her pale hips in black.

She kicked away her pants. "I love thongs."

"*Dios mío,* so do I," he muttered.

"I never wore them until recently. Sometimes when

I'm walking around the city, just running errands, my thong…" She trailed off, reaching for a hair clip.

"Yes?" He held his breath in anticipation.

She twisted her hair and fastened it to the top of her head, her breasts swaying. She gave him a mysterious smile.

She slid her hand over the curve of one breast, drawing languid circles around her nipple. Her hand slipped lower over the soft ivory skin of her belly, stopping just above the scalloped black lace of her thong.

Marco couldn't stifle a groan. He started to get up from the bench and she lifted her hand away from the tiny panties.

"I forgot what I was going to say." She furrowed her brow in mock puzzlement.

"Try to remember," he said, grinding out the words. She was killing him. He sat gingerly, adjusting his painfully erect cock and throbbing testicles.

She dipped her finger under the band of black lace, pulling it away from her slick golden curls. "It rubs the sensitive nub between my legs, up and down, back and forth. Yesterday I was shopping in Marshall Field's and got really hot and aroused. I went into a fitting room."

"What did you do then?" If she had pleasured herself in a public dressing room, he would lose any shred of self-control and explode before she touched him.

She walked past him and opened the door to the sauna. "The room was like this, small and private." She turned and beckoned to him.

He leaped off the bench and followed her inside, mesmerized by the creamy buttocks framed in black. "Did you touch yourself?"

"I thought about it." She gave him a sultry smile. "But I decided to wait until I got home to you."

Home to him. He stopped dead in the doorway, blind-sided by her turn of phrase. No one had ever come home to him.

She dipped the ladle in the bucket and tossed water on the heater in the corner. Steam enveloped them in an intimate haze. "Sit, Marco."

He sat.

She knelt in front of him wearing only her thong. Her arms pushed her breasts together right in front of his cock. She licked her rosy lips, leaving a sexy sheen on them. His breath caught in his chest at the thought of her lips on him. He broke into a sweat that had nothing to do with the sauna's temperature.

"Too hot in here for you?" Steam condensed and dripped off her pink nipples like dew on a rose petal.

"Never." He wouldn't embarrass himself by losing control and exploding all over her bare breasts, but his resolve was sorely tested when she swirled her tongue around the fleshy head of his shaft.

"Mmm." She licked her lips and blew on his damp flesh, causing him to bite back a groan. "I did a little research on Cuban customs on the Internet."

"Research?" His fingers ached from digging into the wooden bench. He'd probably have to pick splinters out from under his nails.

"It was very interesting." Her cool fingers gently cupped and squeezed his balls.

"Okay." His cock twitched upward, wanting her mouth on him.

She laughed triumphantly, obviously enjoying her

sexual power over him. She sat on her heels and swirled a finger around her pale pink nipple. "I found a Web site that mentioned a sexual position called '*la cubana.*'"

"What?" He couldn't have heard right.

"It's supposed to be the hottest thing a woman can do for a man. Have you ever done it Cuban-style?"

He'd heard older boys bragging about it when he'd lived in Cuba but had never done it himself. "No, I never got that lucky."

"Well, *Señor* Flores, today's your lucky day." Before he could tell her every day with her was his lucky day, she leaned over him and pressed a breast on either side of his cock, still slippery from her saliva. She rose, the firm flesh of her breasts molding and squeezing him as if he was plunging deep inside her. Groaning, he leaned his head against the sauna wall, her tight nipples rubbing against his stomach.

Her breasts pressed the length of his shaft as she moved up and down. He gritted his teeth, loving the sight of how she was getting him off. She was getting turned on, too, her breath quickening as her long nipples rubbed through the hair on his belly.

He rolled the peaks between his fingers. She moaned and tried to wiggle away, but she couldn't back up without losing her sexy grip on his cock. "Marco, it'll be my turn later. This is especially for you."

Just then she melted his resistance as quickly as a snowball in the sauna. He watched in agonizing fascination as she lowered her chin.

He groaned as the brick-red head of his cock disappeared between her plump pink lips. Her warm, wet mouth welcomed him, sucking and licking until he let go of her nipples and succumbed to her erotic ministrations.

Around and around she swirled her tongue, pulling him deep into her throat, his aching shaft pulsing against her firm ivory flesh. His balls bumped against the underside of her breasts.

She released him for a second and a growl tore from his throat. The sight of his glistening head was almost too much for him to handle.

"You're so close." Her voice was low and hypnotic, her eyes a narrow rim of blue around her dilated black pupils. "I can taste your juices welling up under my tongue. Your cock is swelling against my breasts."

He thrust upward into her plump lips and firm flesh, almost falling off the bench. A whirlpool of sensation threatened to drown him. She lapped frantically at his head and pressed a hidden bundle of nerves behind his balls he never knew existed. It was too much. His existence had shrunk to her, his Reina, his queen. Her mouth and breasts against his cock. Her tight nipples against his belly. Her fingers against his sac. The waves of his orgasm crashed over him and he spurted into her warm mouth, her clever tongue milking him dry.

He finally opened his eyes and blinked to clear the haze of desire and steam. Rey sat on her heels, smiling at him with such caring that his throat momentarily closed.

"Come here, *corazón*." He pulled her onto his lap, undoing her hair clip and running his fingers through her silky hair.

She curved her lush body around him, her full bottom rubbing on his still-pulsing cock. "Did you like that, Marco?"

"Like that? Any more of that and I would have melted onto your floor."

She giggled and tipped her head back, her long hair
spilling over his arm. "It's amazing what you can find
online."

"God bless the Internet." He was actually stirring
to life under her as her slick breasts pushed against
his chest.

"I'm surprised you never did it that way before."

He cupped her breast, reveling in the weight and heft
against his palm. "No. No one has ever been so generous to me."

Generous? Rey didn't think it was a hardship to have
a muscular, gorgeous man strain against her and play
with her nipples as she sucked on his delicious penis.
As if he read her thoughts, he rolled her nipple between
his fingers, pulling it to an impossible length. She managed to gasp, "I enjoy watching you lose control." It was
easier to say that than tell him about the strange mix of
affection and tenderness that she'd felt as he'd cried her
name in the midst of his orgasm.

"Control?" He flipped her under him and spread her
knees wide. "We'll see who loses control now."

"Just try it," she dared him, her breathing rapid and
aroused.

"Oh, I will." He sucked her nipple deep into his
mouth, laving her pliant flesh until she shuddered. "How
many times do you want to come? Two or three?"

"Four." Self-control was highly overrated anyway.

MARCO LET THE PHONE IN his brother's apartment ring
while he grabbed some clean clothes. It was probably

one of Francisco's girlfriends. The machine clicked on and a creaky Cuban voice came through the speaker.

"Francisco Flores, this is *Señora* Ortega, the neighbor of your *mamá*." Marco stared at the machine and leaped across the room to snatch the phone.

"*Señora* Ortega, this is Francisco." The old woman was practically deaf and never could tell the two brothers apart.

"Francisco, you need to come home to Miami right away. Bless the Virgin, no one was killed, and your mother's things were at Luis's house but…" The *señora* rattled on.

"What happened?" Marco could hardly breathe. Had Rodríguez found his mother?

"Some evildoer threw a Russian drink through your *mamá's* front window."

"What?" For a crazy instant Marco had an image of a vodka shot glass spiraling through the air. "You mean a Molotov cocktail?"

"*Sí*, that is what the man from the fire department said. I told him your *mamá* is on her honeymoon cruise with Luis, so you and your brother have to come fix the house. It is black from all the smoke and fire, but it didn't burn down. Where is Marco anyway?"

Right here in Chicago. "I think he's in Europe." Marco's stomach churned at the memory of how hard his mother had worked to buy her house, a widow in a strange country with two fatherless boys.

"Europe is too far. You have to come home, young man. Your *mamá* is on her honeymoon and shouldn't be disturbed."

"I can't come to Miami. I'm in the middle of a job."

The old lady's sharp disapproval radiated through the phone line. He actually cringed. No *proper* Cuban son would ignore such a summons.

"Francisco Ignacio Flores." Her voice shook with indignation. "I won't ruin your mother's trip, but you can be sure that she will hear about this when she comes home."

"I'm very sorry, *señora*. If I could come home, I would. I think my mother will understand." If she didn't kill him herself once she realized the danger he'd put them all in. He hadn't told her anything about his latest investigation, knowing that she'd be away if the *mierda* hit the fan.

"You young men. Not a thought in your head about *la familia,* only work and women. I won't forget this, Francisco, and neither will any of your mother's friends." She hung up with a loud click.

Marco was left with a dial tone. The rage that had simmered through his veins for the past two decades boiled over and he slammed his fist into the wall, knocking a hole in the cheap Sheetrock. Rodríguez was using his family as bait to draw him home to Miami, home to a certain death.

Marco stared blankly at the torn skin on his bleeding knuckles. Not for the first time, he bitterly regretted his inability to protect his family. The drug lord had the balls to harm his mother a second time. After Marco got through with him, Rodríguez wouldn't have any balls at all.

11

"THAT'S ENOUGH FOR TODAY, Marco. You've been posing all afternoon."

He stretched his shoulders and pulled on his robe while she fretted over her latest effort.

"Since we're at the two-week point in the project, Evelyn wants to see at least a dozen sketches."

He walked behind her and examined her sketches. "They're fantastic. Something you'd see in a museum."

"A museum? Hardly," Rey scoffed, secretly pleased. His compliment jogged her memory, though, and she glanced at the calendar. Was it already Friday? "Actually, I have tickets to a gala opening tonight at the Art Institute of Chicago. Would you like to come with me?"

"I've never been to a gala opening. What's the occasion?"

"They're unveiling a recently rediscovered statue by Michelangelo." She'd been so wrapped up in her own living, breathing version of Michelangelo's *David* that she'd almost forgotten the event she'd been looking forward to for weeks.

"Now even *I've* heard of him." His caramel eyes twinkled.

"My absolute favorite artist. I saw his statues in Italy when I was a teenager and knew I had to be a sculptor, too."

"Even then you liked looking at naked men."

"What?" she sputtered. "Nude statues are an important genre of classical art, dating back to the ancient Greeks and continuing through modern times."

He grinned and held up his hands. "Take it easy. I was just kidding." He grabbed her around the waist, squeezing her bottom in his big hands. "I don't mind you looking at naked men."

"Good." She smiled at him, enjoying his sensual massage. His obvious appreciation of her ass had eased her self-consciousness. "Because once we finish our project, I'll have to hire other nude models to fit my new commissions."

His grip tightened, his face darkening. "Correction. I don't mind you looking at *me* naked. As for those other models, they can go to hell."

Rey pushed out of his arms, staring at his clenched jaw. "You're jealous? This is what I do for a living, and I'm damn good at it. Do you think I hop into the sack with every male model I hire?"

He ran his fingers through his hair and took a deep breath. "Sorry. I know you don't do that." He paced over to the coffeemaker and poured himself a cup, leaning his hips against the countertop. "Like you said, it's how you earn your living."

"Not much of one." Since he'd apologized, she decided not to make a big deal of his possessiveness. Maybe all Cuban men had that tendency.

"What do you mean?" He sipped his coffee elegantly, his large brown pinky finger curving incongruously from the tiny demitasse handle.

"The Bucktown neighborhood is a hot real-estate market. My building is being turned into condos, so I have to either buy my apartment or move out."

"Where would you live?" He set down the cup, his eyes intense.

The logistics of moving all her artwork as well as her personal belongings would be a nightmare. "Probably a one-bedroom apartment. I'd have to rent storage space and find somewhere else to do my artwork. That's why this commission is so important. If I don't produce a big chunk of cash for a down payment, I won't qualify for a mortgage." She crossed next to him and poured herself a big cup.

"Take it easy on that coffee. You'll be awake all night."

"If I can't sleep, will you stay up with me?" She stroked him through the robe flap. His breath came out in a hiss. She rubbed her breasts against his chest and he grabbed her wrist.

"Part of me will be up all night." His erection pressed against her hand before he let go. "But tell me about the new statue at the museum."

"The statue is actually almost five hundred years old and is called *Adam Banished from Paradise*. The Russians recently found it in a cache of artwork liberated from Rome in the last days of World War II." Rey laid heavy emphasis on the word *liberated*. Thousands of paintings and statues had been stolen during the chaos of war.

He frowned. "Damned Communists. They steal everything that's not nailed down."

Okay, another sore spot. He sure had a lot. "No one's seen the statue in sixty years except for old black-and-white photos in art history books, but we can finally see him."

"Him?" Marco asked.

Rey's face grew warm. "I, um, have a tendency to anthropomorphize great works of art. I don't like to call such a beautiful thing 'it.'"

"'A thing of beauty is a joy forever, it will never pass into nothingness.'" He reddened slightly, as if embarrassed.

Rey stared at him. "That was wonderful. It's exactly how I feel." The poetic words seemed at odds with his intense personality and athletic, scarred body.

He avoided her gaze. "Don't give me so much credit. An English poet named Keats wrote those lines in *Endymion* almost two hundred years ago."

"So you like poetry?" That would teach Rey not to assume he was uneducated just because he was modeling for a living.

He shrugged. "My father read poetry to us when we were young. He was a professor of English literature at the university in Havana."

"And you said he died right before you left Cuba?"

"Yes. He got sick and didn't get any medical care." He clenched his jaw and looked away, his gaze seeing something or someone who wasn't in the room.

"Marco?" She touched his arm lightly. Something seemed strange. Didn't Cuba boast of an excellent health-care system?

"I have to go to my apartment. I didn't bring anything that would work for an art gala." He pulled on his briefs and found his pants flung over a corner of her drawing table.

"What you're wearing is fine. Black is the clothing color of choice of the art world."

"No. I have to go." He pulled on his coat and kissed her fiercely. The metal door shut with a clang behind him.

She didn't know what to think. His mood was becoming harder and darker, only lightening when they made love. Wait. *Had sex.* She blinked hard. Made love? Where had that come from? Was she falling in love with her mysterious model?

"*SEÑOR,* OUR SOURCE HAS located Flores's brother." Gabriel slid the file across the polished wooden expanse of his desk. "Although *Señora* Flores was unharmed, being out of the country on her honeymoon, she did leave an emergency phone number with her elderly neighbor."

"And?"

"One of our men posed as an insurance adjuster and got the phone number. The younger brother is apparently living in Chicago."

"Hmm. If we can get the brother, Flores will beg us to take him instead." Rodríguez rolled his golden pen between his fingers, remembering how the younger boy had squealed from just a few shallow cuts. No wonder he had grown up to be a pansy. "Our contacts in Chicago are too well-known to the police."

"Yes, *patrón,* I've made arrangements to send our own men from Miami."

"Who?"

His assistant looked away and murmured something.

"Speak up, Gabriel!"

"Chucho and Nico García."

"The García brothers?" Rodríguez sat back in his leather chair. "Why not Sánchez?"

"He caught a fishing hook in his trigger finger in the Keys and has blood poisoning."

"What happened to Rivera?"

"He started a bar fight in Santo Domingo. The judge sentenced him to sixty days."

"And Gómez?"

"Immigration deported him."

"In the entire South Florida area you can't find anyone better than Chucho and Nico?"

His assistant shrugged, his expression anxious. As well it should be. "The Super Bowl is at Pro Player Stadium next week. INS and Metro-Dade PD are cleaning house for the tourists. Unfortunately they've also rounded up our *soldados*."

"All right. Send Chucho and Nico to Chicago to find the brother. Once we have him, Flores will come running."

"*Señor,* your trial starts in three weeks," his assistant reminded him.

"I'll go to Chicago and take care of him myself. It will be a pleasure after all these years." Rodríguez pushed to his feet and walked over to a floral arrangement in an Italian marble urn on a pedestal.

Huge fleshy lilies with lush, jutting stamens were his favorites. He swirled the yellow pollen around his finger, jamming it deep into the heart of the petals. He didn't know why he bothered to fertilize the flower. It was already dead but didn't know it. Just like Flores.

12

"LET'S GO INTO THE MUSEUM. THE exhibit should open soon." Rey looked up at the facade of the Art Institute of Chicago, its fifty-foot marble columns shining white against the black Chicago night. Nostalgia rolled over her. "I went to college here."

"At the museum?" His baritone voice was muffled through the scarf.

"The Art Institute has its own art school. I was lucky enough to be accepted."

"Lucky? Or were you talented and hardworking?"

Rey had never thought of it like that. "My mother was very opposed to me attending art school. If I had painted misty watercolors of French gardens, that would have been marginally acceptable. But to sculpt heavy blocks of stone, muck around with clay—no way. Especially of naked men! The horror of it. My mother's friends all wondered if I was a slut."

"You could never be a slut."

Prior to Marco, she'd been celibate for months. "Maybe a sex fiend."

"Lucky for me." He winked.

She grinned back. "My mother wanted me to get my M.R.S. degree at Northwestern or University of

Chicago, preferably the school with the most rich guys."

He furrowed what she could see of his forehead. "I'm not familiar with that degree."

"M.R.S. just spells *Mrs.* To graduate with an engagement ring you need to major in sorority parties, fraternity dances and stalking prelaw and premed students."

"Is it important for you to be with a man with all sorts of degrees?" He asked the question casually, looking at the pair of ten-foot-high marble lions guarding the museum entrance.

"I've met so many morons with law or medical degrees that I think formal education can be highly overrated. The doctors and lawyers were my mother's ideal, not mine."

He squeezed her hand. "And what do you want?"

"What do I want?" She paused to marshal her thoughts. "I want to make my own choices. For the past several years I've only pleased other people. 'What kind of painting would you like?' 'How big should the sculpture be?' 'That's okay, I didn't need to have an orgasm tonight.'" She slapped a mittened hand over her mouth. That last one had just slipped out.

Marco stopped dead in his tracks, ignoring the pushing crowds on Michigan Avenue. "I hope you didn't stay with such a selfish man."

Her shoulders slumped briefly. "Actually, I did for several months. I was inexperienced sexually and he told me my lack of fulfillment was my fault."

"Bastardo." He spit out a few more Spanish curses.

Rey tugged him along and they merged into the busy pedestrian traffic. It was easier to talk about Stefan if she was moving and not looking into Marco's eyes. "When

I finally got the nerve to break it off, he told me I was as lousy in the art studio as I was in the bedroom."

"What?" Waves of anger rolled off him.

"It's okay, really," she said, forestalling his objections. "I decided to prove everyone wrong."

"And you did." He put his arm around her shoulder. "Reina, I may not be an expert, but your artwork looks great." Marco flicked her icy nose, one of the few body parts visible under her winter clothes. "And as for the bedroom, if you get any better, I may not survive until February. You are the hottest woman I've ever met. Brains, spirit and body."

She laughed. "As if you could tell through this thick winter jacket."

He wiggled the dark wings of his eyebrows. "I have a trained memory."

"Who trained it?" Not for the first time she wondered about his background. Even after her coaching, his modeling skills needed a lot of work. She hoped he had a backup plan.

"Years of looking at beautiful women." Halfway up the white marble steps leading to the museum lobby, the stiletto heel of her expensive leather boot slipped on a patch of ice. She flailed briefly before he steadied her. "Are you okay?"

"I'm fine." She wasn't used to anyone saving her, even from something as minor as falling in the snow.

"Good." The crowds pushed them along through the elaborate ironwork doors into the soaring lobby. They picked their way through the puddles of melting snow on the slick terrazzo floors to the coat check.

After checking their coats, they turned the corner.

Despite the frigid weather, the gallery was packed. It had been years since Michelangelo's works had come to the United States, let alone a sculpture lost for sixty years.

Art students in unrelieved black hunched over sketch pads and pencils. As they slowly circled the seven-foot marble, their Doc Martens narrowly avoided the Manolo-shod feet of Chicago society doyennes. The ladies' winter wool pantsuits ranging from eggshell to taupe skimmed over their uplifted breasts and tucked tummies. Rey smiled. She hadn't seen so many blondes in one room since her last trip to Sweden. Number thirty-four, Light Ash Blonde. It was her mother's favorite shade because it looked natural and did an absolutely fabulous job of covering the gray.

Rey wiggled through the crowd until she saw the Michelangelo sculpture for the first time. Its ivory glow blurred in her vision for an instant, and she swallowed past the lump in her throat. She walked towards the marble as if she were approaching a church altar, the gallery's dull murmur fading. She stopped behind the barrier and looked up.

"Oh, my God." Her tone was reverent. Michelangelo's soul leaped out from the marble figure of Adam, naked save for a fig-leaf apron. She circled it slowly, devouring its elegance and power. The five-hundred-year-old Carrara marble glowed as if lit from within, the smooth stone curving flawlessly into muscle, bone and sinew. The tendons and ligaments of his fingers clawed to keep Heaven in their grasp, and his anguished eyes strove for one last glimpse of earthly paradise. Rey almost saw the tear tracks on the statue's face. God's own creation, banished from earthly paradise. Adam twisted in a pose of agony, his upper body turned to face the Garden gates lost to him forever.

Rey reached out to touch it but clasped her hands together instead. She blinked as tears filled her eyes and spilled down her cheeks. A warm pair of hands gripped her shoulders.

"Are you all right?" Marco murmured, his warm breath fanning her ear.

She couldn't answer him immediately. Her emotions churned. Joy at the statue's beauty, sorrow for its anguish and awe that Michelangelo bound so much power and passion into a chunk of rock.

"If I had only a fraction, only one-thousandth of his talent, I would be the happiest artist in the world," she choked out. "To have the skill to do this." She swiped at a tear and clasped her hands again.

He caressed her shoulders, running his hands down to her elbows. "Why are you gripping your hands together?"

She gave a watery laugh. She released her hands and turned to face him. With her high-heeled boots on, his sympathetic eyes were level with her tear-blurred ones.

"To keep myself from touching the statue. To feel what Michelangelo felt, to follow the curves of his chisel." She smiled. "Of course, no one's allowed to touch the artwork. The oils and acids on human skin damage the marble. Under normal circumstances the security guards scold anyone who touches the artwork, but with a Michelangelo they'd probably march me out the door and throw me into Lake Michigan."

Marco watched her solemnly, his eyes never leaving

hers. "I know a better way to keep your hands occupied." He took her chilly left hand in his, bringing it to his mouth. The warm press of his kiss burned her palm. She stared at him, shocked that a simple kiss roiled her emotions. His suave manner slipped a notch and he smiled crookedly. "Now you can examine this amazing statue without worrying about an icy swim."

She moved as close as the red velvet barrier ropes allowed, still conscious of her arm pressed against the hot silk of Marco's side. She quelled her sexual response to him and avoided his gaze.

Now that the wave of her emotional response had crested, Rey examined the statue with a more objective eye. The tension flowed through the muscular thighs, buttocks and back, culminating in the cords of his neck supporting a perfectly shaped head.

"La figura serpentinata," she murmured to herself.

"The serpentine figure?" Marco asked. His voice startled her from her reverie. He had understood her mumbled Italian, so like his native Spanish.

"Oh, um…" She had to collect her thoughts for a second. "Michelangelo created that concept. The serpentine figure is a small head on a muscular torso flowing into tapering thighs. The whole body twists in a serpentine manner to emphasize a combination of power and elegance." Rey couldn't help looking at Marco's own heavily muscled chest and abdomen. His thighs also bore a certain resemblance to the statue. "Actually, your body looks a lot like this statue," she blurted. Marco grinned and she blushed.

A beige-suited socialite overheard her and appraised Marco's body. Judging from her wide, professionally whitened smile, the eavesdropper was mentally stripping off his tight-fitting gray silk pullover and slim-cut black pants.

Rey glared at her, and the older woman sauntered off, her gaze lingering on Marco's ass.

"Why such a fierce look?" he asked.

"Someone was eavesdropping on our conversation."

"Which part?"

"The part about how Michelangelo invented the idea of the serpentine figure," she lied.

"Art lovers can be so rude." He knew exactly which comment that old bag had overheard.

Rey turned toward the statue, determined to focus on its beauty. Marco stepped behind her and whispered, "Thank you for the compliment. There's just one problem."

Her stomach sank. She'd offended him, first yapping on about his body and then acting overprotective and jealous. "What?"

"You know I don't have a small head." He grinned slyly. "Either one of them."

Rey stifled a giggle and turned away briefly to regain her self-control. The society matron with the wandering eye was approaching them. Rey stared hard at the woman's face.

"Oh, no." She clenched her jaw. "It's Honey Van Der Waal, my mother's old friend."

"Her name is Honey?"

"It ought to be Vinegar. She tried to get my dad into her bed for years. Fortunately he only had eyes for my mother. Here she comes."

"Rey? Is that you? How are you?" Honey air-kissed Rey's cheek. "It's been so long!"

Not long enough. "Honey! What a surprise. I didn't know you liked Michelangelo."

She waved a diamond-encrusted hand negligently. "I've always been an Art Institute patron, darling. Besides, you know how I love looking at fabulous naked men."

Rey bristled. The battle-ax made Michelangelo's *Adam* sound like an all-boy revue on Rush Street.

"And who is your friend?"

"Honey, this is Marco. Marco, Honey Van Der Waal is one of my mother's *old* friends."

Honey's eyes narrowed slightly and she extended her hand to Marco, palm down. Rey's arm dropped as Marco took Honey's bejeweled claw. For one sickening second Rey thought Marco would kiss the back of Honey's hand. She didn't want to admit how relieved she was when he only bowed slightly in a European manner.

Rey stared at the statue over Honey's shoulder, hoping the woman would get the hint and leave them alone. Without thinking about it, she clasped her hands in front of her again.

"*Querida,* let me do that." Marco took her hand and laced his strong brown fingers between hers. He turned slightly to the side, forcing Honey to shuffle in front of them.

"And Rey, how are Brigitte and Hans?"

"My parents are fine. Traveling where it's warm."

"You be sure to tell them hello the next time they call." Honey turned to Marco with a little laugh. "Rey's mother and I quite despaired of her. She was a plump little thing always grubbing around with clay."

Rey opened her mouth to cut Honey down to size

when Marco stepped in. "Actually, Rey is quite a talented artist. Her newest commission will put her on the map."

"Well, dear, don't let dabbling in art interfere with finding an eligible young man. My son Grayson recently got engaged, so there's one less bachelor to go around."

Ugh. She hoped the future ex–Mrs. Grayson Van Der Waal had a good prenup.

"And what do you do, Marco?" She turned her back to Rey and smiled toothily at him.

"I work for Rey." He covered Rey's hand with his.

Honey's eyebrows twitched up as far as her BO-TOXed forehead would let her.

Rey groaned inwardly. Honey thought Marco was a gigolo. "Marco is an artist's model."

The older woman smirked. "Really? I've always wanted to take up art. Perhaps you can model for me."

He leaned into Rey's side. "Rey keeps me very busy, so I won't be free to take on other projects."

"If you're ever dissatisfied with Rey's, uh, output, let me know." She pressed a business card into Marco's palm. Not bothering to air-kiss Rey, she sauntered off.

Rey fumed. "The only thing she paints is her face. She's too stupid to count high enough for paint-by-numbers."

"What was that about not liking eligible men?"

Rey grimaced. "Her son Grayson had a liking for 'plump little things who grubbed around in clay.' Unfortunately he chose to express his affection by cornering me at a high school party. When he grabbed my breasts, I punched him in the nose."

"Good for you."

"Lifting heavy chunks of stone made me stronger than I thought. Grayson's nose was shoved halfway to his ear. He and Honey had a mother-son special deal at the plastic surgeon for new noses. I wish I hadn't punched him."

"Don't feel sorry for scumbags like that, Rey. They never deserve your pity." His face was stony as he gripped her hand.

"No, I sprained my wrist when I hit him. I had to wear an elastic bandage for two weeks and couldn't do any artwork."

Marco looked at her in surprise and gave a big belly laugh that echoed up to the twenty-foot ceiling. "Next time use your knee. It's bigger and stronger."

"I'll have to remember that."

"If I'm around, you won't have to," he promised.

She smiled, warmth curling through her. The cozy feeling stayed as she stared at the statue for long minutes. Marco stood patiently with her, nodding as she pointed out tiny details only a professional sculptor would notice.

She left him in the gallery while she used the ladies' room downstairs. She washed her hands and left, eager to find him and show him her favorite Renaissance paintings. She turned the corner and bumped into another one of the black-garbed artistic souls that drooped around the museum.

"Excuse me." She walked past and stiffened when the man caught her arm.

"Freya, dear." His unctuous tones slithered along her spine. Only one man disgusted her so thoroughly with just two words. She tugged her arm free.

"Stefan." Rey announced his name with all the enthusiasm of finding a flaming bag of dog doo on her doorstep. "First of all, no one calls me Freya. And I am definitely not your 'dear.'"

He ignored her words, just as he always had. "It's been so long since we talked."

Not long enough. She'd purposely stayed away from gallery openings for years before she gathered the courage to even be in the same room with him. She'd avoided talking to him until now. But no more. What could he say to sting her now?

She took a deep breath. "What brings you to the Michelangelo exhibit, Stefan? Did the craft store run out of Popsicle sticks?"

Stefan's pasty complexion reddened at her mention of his last exhibition, where he'd painted Popsicle sticks thirty different colors and thrown them willy-nilly on the gallery floor, supposedly to symbolize the randomness of life. The *Chicago Tribune* art critic had not been kind. "At least I try to expand my horizons, to free myself from the bourgeois constraints of the dreary past." He stroked his yellowish gray goatee, obviously waiting for her expressions of awe.

Rey laughed outright. He still sounded as he had ten years ago. No wonder he only dated impressionable teenagers. Anyone over twenty-one would see right through his bullshit. "And the art museum is a good place to get free from the dreary past?"

He stepped toward her, a sneer twisting his narrow face. "That's the problem you've always had, Freya. Your work is hackneyed and cheap."

Rey stood toe-to-toe with him, her blood churning with rage. She refused to let this pathetic little man intimidate her anymore. "Cheap? This from a man who tried to sell a collection of Popsicle sticks for two thousand dollars? I just got a commission to sculpt a block of Carrara marble for six figures, Stefan. So you can stick that up your narrow ass along with your Popsicle sticks."

He grabbed her upper arms and squeezed painfully. "Listen, you little bitch, I'll destroy you, I swear."

Rey'd had enough. She raised her Jimmy Choo boot and ground the stiletto heel into Stefan's thin leather loafer.

Fortunately he wasn't part of the Doc Martens crowd, she thought, as he let go and hopped in place, clutching his foot.

Gray strands flopped loose from the leather thong binding his hair, and he shoved them back from his face and raised his fist. She knew he meant to hit her and stepped away, but the wall was behind her. Before he got close enough, she kicked him in the knee as hard as she could, the edge of her boot connecting with a satisfying thud. When he hunched over in pain, he was still crowding her, so she kneed him in the face and darted past.

She was free, her breath coming fast and strong.

Stefan staggered against the wall. "By node." His voice was muffled behind his hands. "I dink you broke it."

"If you ever touch me again, I'll make you even less of a man." Her words came out as steely as her chisel. Triumph rushed over her, the long-held memories of Stefan's criticisms disappearing in her rush of victory.

"What the hell is going on?" Marco stood between her and Stefan. His voice was deceptively calm, but his eyes narrowed and his fists clenched against his sides. "Reina, did this man attack you?"

Rey got a thrill from seeing Stefan cower. "I took care of Stefan."

"You took care of him?" A muscle ticked in his jaw. "Now it's my turn." Marco looked ready to tear him apart.

She was tempted to let him, but a one-sided ass-kicking on the Art Institute's lower level would undoubtedly attract attention. And with everyone in the Chicago art scene upstairs, well, that would be poor career planning on her part. She touched Marco's tense forearm. "No, he won't bother me anymore." He relaxed slightly, but the danger still coiled close to the surface. "I don't want you to get into any trouble over him."

"No trouble, Rey." She couldn't figure out how he'd done it. One second he stood next to her and the next second he was hustling Stefan into the men's room. "I'm just going to help him clean up his bloody nose."

Right. She stood alone, rubbing the bruises on her upper arms and flexing her sore toes inside her trusty boot. Stefan had denigrated her for the last time. And whatever Marco was going to do, it was where the museum officials couldn't see.

13

MARCO PROPELLED THE GREASY little man by the scruff of his neck into the empty men's room. "Let's get some of that blood off your face. It's ugly enough as it is." Stefan dug his heels in and skittered along the gray terrazzo floor. Marco ignored his wimpy struggles and hustled him around the corner. He'd dropped men twice Stefan's size. He eyeballed the dirtbag's skinny body. No, make that three times his size.

The sleazeball took refuge in a haughty manner. Too bad he had blood and snot dripping down his face. "How dare you lay your hands on me! Do you know who I am?"

"I know you're a man who lays your hands on women." Marco strove to speak normally, anger clenching his throat closed. Who the hell was this *pendejo* and why had he grabbed Rey?

"You know how women are, right, buddy?" Stefan tried to slide by, but Marco shoved him into the tile wall.

"No. Tell me."

The older man's eyes darted around the washroom, but Marco shifted his weight to block the exit. "They don't know what they want, always saying no when they mean yes."

Rage crashed through Marco like a breaker on the beach. He grabbed Stefan's collar and shoved him under the faucet. Instead of Stefan's narrow face, he saw *El Lobo*'s smirk, his grimy hands as he had reached for Marco's *mamá*.

"I never touched her," Stefan gasped as the water poured into his mouth. Pink water stained the white sink basin and swirled down the drain.

"So she's a liar?" It was hard to understand his gargling noises, so Marco dug his fingers into a wet fistful of gray hair and pulled the greasy bastard up. He was a sorry sight. Marco grimaced as Stefan sniffled and wiped a black sleeve across his dripping nose.

"Yes, no, I mean…" the older man sputtered as Marco pushed him under the water again. His head made a satisfying thunk against the faucet. Marco pulled him up and shoved him against a urinal.

Stefan darted a glance at the door. "Look, man, whatever we had was a long time ago. She wasn't even that memorable, if you know what I mean."

This man dared to speak like this of his beautiful Reina? Marco wanted to hurt him, break his ribs until every breath was agony, punch his kidneys until he pissed blood.

He drew a deep breath, realizing that Rey wouldn't want him to make trouble for her. "Look, *maricón*, if I ever catch you bothering Rey or any other woman, I'll strangle you with your own ponytail." He whispered a few more evil threats that he'd learned from his days in the cartel. Stefan blanched. *"¿Comprende?"*

"I understand." Stefan straightened slowly. When he realized Marco wasn't going to hit him, he scuttled out, his stacked heels sliding on the puddles of water. Marco washed his hands and dried them on a paper towel. Blood speckled the sink basin. "Out, out, damn spot," he murmured to himself and stared into the mirror. The lust for vengeance still roiled through him. Had his time with hardened criminals twisted him into a violent man?

"WHAT ON EARTH DID YOU do to him?" Rey asked. Stefan had refused to meet her stare and had given her a wide berth as he'd left the men's room. Marco hadn't given him any visible bruises or broken bones. Unfortunately.

"Nothing. I helped him wash the blood off his face. Blood that you put there, by the way."

She smiled, pleased with herself. "He deserved it, grabbing me and backing me into a corner. I defended myself pretty well, don't you think?"

"You were *magnífica*." He kissed her cheek as they walked away from the restrooms. "I never knew Swedes were such brawlers."

She giggled. "Not since Viking times. Swedes are pretty low-key. We haven't even fought since the Napoleonic Wars."

Marco laughed with her and took her hand, peering at her knuckles. "No marks on you."

She grinned at him. "I might have a small bruise on my knee, but that's all."

"A knee strike?" He pulled her against him as they turned the corner leading to the stairs. "You took my advice."

"Yes, I didn't want to hurt my hands. I only have another week to finish those preliminary sketches and I can't afford any downtime."

He roared with laughter. "Good for you. Did you kick him, too?"

She stuck one foot out in front of her and wiggled her boot. "I've even got the sore toes to prove it."

"Poor toes. Maybe I can give you a foot rub when we get home." They climbed the stairs holding hands.

Home. She liked the sound of that word coming out of his mouth. Maybe too much, in fact. He was hers only until their job was done. And if she wanted a home to, well, come home to, she had to work hard for it. She wouldn't forget that fact. "Let's go to the European painting galleries so I can show you Mars, god of war."

"Marco is the Spanish version of the Latin name Marcus, after the god of war."

"Really? That makes sense." She grimaced. "I guess I should tell you the expanded definition of Freya. Goddess of springtime, love and, um, fertility."

"No kidding?" They were at the top of the stairs, and he clasped her other hand, as well. "The god of war meets the goddess of love. Have you descended from Viking heaven to counteract my dark side?"

"Viking heaven is called Valhalla, and no, I don't think you have a dark side."

"Oh, I'm no angel." A muscle ticked along his jaw.

"Lucky for me." She strove for a light tone to counteract his grim one.

He looked at her, a serious expression on his face. "I've done some things I'm not proud of."

"We all have. I just beat up a prominent local artist in the Art Institute's basement." She couldn't help but laugh, not just at the memory of Stefan's bloody nose but also at the lightness that came from confronting a painful part of her past.

"I mean it, Rey. If you knew, you wouldn't laugh."

"What did you do, kill someone?" she joked.

There was a long silence. She turned to look at him in surprise. His response was taking just a little too long.

"No. No, I never killed anyone." He stared straight ahead, his profile set in rigid lines.

Rey pulled him into the hall of Renaissance painters. One towering masterpiece of the Spanish painter El Greco's soared over the lofty gallery. "Are you a religious man, Marco?"

"I used to be." His expression was grim.

"Look at the saints and sinners in the paintings. See how the light of heaven falls equally on them?" Whatever mysterious guilt he carried was eating him up.

His gaze followed her finger and he stared at the huge paintings.

"Whatever you did is in the past. Let the light in."

He said some words in Spanish.

"What did you say?" she asked.

"*Luz de mi vida.* Light of my life."

"That's exactly what I mean. Let some light into your life."

He swept her into his arms, murmuring, "No, Reina. You are the *luz de mi vida.*"

"THIS IS YOUR CAPTAIN speaking. On behalf of all our crew, thank you for flying Air Florida. We will be landing in Chicago's O'Hare International Airport in approximately ten minutes. The seat-belt light is on."

Nico eyed his younger brother, Chucho, who was

shifting in discomfort. "Maybe if you cut back on the fried bananas and pork roasts, you'd fit in the seat."

"It's a good thing this flight is nonsmoking. Otherwise all that grease in your hair would catch fire," Chucho sneered.

"At least I have hair. You can shave your head all you want—you're still bald," Nico said.

"Local time is 11:35 p.m. and local temperature is a balmy ten degrees." The captain clicked off the microphone.

Chucho elbowed Nico. "Ten degrees? That's not so bad."

"That's ten degrees Fahrenheit, *idiota!*" Nico hissed.

"Don't call me an idiot. I'm not the one speaking Spanish like *el jefe* told us not to."

The flight attendant gave them a suspicious look as she pushed the beverage cart past, so they subsided sullenly into their seats.

"Excuse me." The flight attendant leaned over.

Chucho gave her his version of a charming smile, highlighting his golden incisor. "Yes?"

"Please fasten your seat belts. We'll be landing shortly." She bustled off, ignoring them for the rest of the flight.

"Her ass is too skinny anyway," Chucho grumbled.

They managed to disembark and leave the airport without attracting security, which Nico considered a major accomplishment, considering his younger brother's tendency to shoot off at the mouth.

"*Dios mío!*" Nico gasped. "I've never been so cold in my life. Let's find a taxi before my *cojones* freeze off." Cold air knifed through his thin leather coat.

"They're small enough already." Chucho jammed his hands into his pockets and hunched his shoulders.

"Big enough to be in charge of finding Flores," Nico jibed, hailing a cab. "And big enough to be in charge of you."

14

REY TWIRLED HER CHARCOAL stick between her fingers. She alternated between staring at Marco and staring at her sketch pad. Her sketch was just crap. She sighed. "You can relax for a minute, Marco."

He lifted his right foot off the box he was posing on. "What is it, Reina?"

"Nothing looks right today." She tossed the charcoal on her drawing table, not even caring that it left a big smudge against the paper.

"Do you want me to change position?" He flexed his chest and shoulders, getting ready to hold another pose.

"No, you're doing a great job. Much more comfortable with posing and modeling. It's me. I can't draw a fluid, relaxed line to save my life today."

He walked behind her and put his hands on her shoulders. "No wonder. Your muscles are hard as rocks." He dug his thumbs into her shoulder blades.

She moaned in delight, rolling her neck. Her vertebrae popped as he rubbed his palms along her spine.

"I got here at eleven, and it's almost seven o'clock. You deserve a break after working so many hours."

Rey grinned and leaned into his warm chest. "First

of all, you got here at eleven, but you came at noon, remember?"

He growled playfully and slipped his hands around her rib cage to cup her breasts. "And you came at eleven-ten, eleven-thirty and noon." He played with the tips of her nipples, pulling them into aching points. "Then we worked for three hours and took another break when your agent called."

Rey grimaced and pulled away. Evelyn not only wanted the sketches of Marco but also requested a small clay mock-up of the final statue within the week. "Aargh! I can't handle this! I'll move out of my loft and go work at Starbucks. I make good coffee, don't I?" She knew she was babbling, but her nerves had gotten the best of her.

"Yes, you do, but I think you've had enough caffeine for today." He kissed the nape of her neck. "Have you seen my pants?"

She pointed to the chaise where they'd flung them almost as soon as he'd walked in the door. Since they'd become lovers, he hadn't bothered changing in the cubicle.

She spotted the black leather bag he usually carried. "Here's your bag." She'd already grabbed a handle when he whipped his head around.

"Leave it." His tone was sharp. He stood and strode over to her wearing only his briefs.

"Oh. Okay." He sure was possessive of his stuff.

He took the bag from her hands but not before she'd hefted it in one hand. "Are you carrying around bricks?"

"No, just books, a change of clothes, some toiletries." He pulled on his brown pants and grabbed a clean camel-colored microfiber T-shirt.

"You look nice." That was an understatement. The T-shirt hugged the curves and valleys of his chest. He tucked the shirt into his waistband and buckled his slim leather belt. Rey was acutely conscious of her gray paint-stained sweatshirt and linty black leggings that bagged at the knee.

"So do you." He crossed over to her and smiled.

"Ha." She suddenly wanted to cry. Her art career teetered on the brink, she'd resorted to sleeping with her stunning male model for inspiration and their no-strings affair had tangled her up in knots.

He must have seen her distress because he pulled her into a hug. "You are the most beautiful woman in the world, Reina."

She sniffled, his heart thudding steadily under her cheek. "I bet you say that to all the female artists you model for."

"No. You're the only one. Ever." He sounded amused. "You need to get out. When was the last time you had fun?"

She raised one golden eyebrow. "Today at noon."

He threw back his head and laughed. "I meant the kind of fun you have in public."

"You can have that kind of fun in public?" Paint-splattered sweatshirt or no, she rubbed her breasts against him.

"Almost, and it's called salsa dancing. Now go put on a tight little dress and some dancing shoes."

She cheered up right away. "I know just the outfit." She'd gone shopping with Meg just last week and had bought a sexy little number. Until Marco, she never would have dared try on a dress like that, much less buy

it. But his obvious appreciation for her curves had boosted her confidence.

So one tight little dress coming up. And later, coming *off*.

15

"BUDDY. HEY, BUDDY. IS THIS the club you wanted?"

Marco dragged his gaze away from Rey's perfect profile. The cabbie was staring at her, too, her glossy red lips shining even in the shadows. He cleared his throat. "This is it, thanks." The rhythmic bongo drumbeat and piercing trumpets of a hot salsa tune pulsed into the street. He'd purposely avoided the club downtown where Francisco tended bar.

He helped Rey out of the cab and paid the driver. The lapels of her black velvet coat parted briefly, showing a long expanse of silk-stockinged thigh. She caught the path of his glance and smiled.

All right. He had to know. "What did you decide to wear?" She'd come out of her room wearing the long cloak-type garment and hadn't let him see what she had picked for their evening of salsa dancing. The only thing she'd said was that her dress was short and tight, just as he'd requested.

"You'll see when we get into the club." She held her jacket closed, her eyes dark and mysterious with some smoky eye shadow.

He put his hand on the small of her back and hustled her into Club Tropical, eager to strip off her coat. The pink-and-green-neon palm trees over the narrow entrance reflected off the golden clip fastening up her hair.

He dragged his stare away from her to scan the crush of club goers. If Rodríguez had sent someone, Marco didn't recognize him.

"Hey, Francisco, *¿qué pasa?*" Marco spun around as a short man in an expensive Italian suit slapped him on the shoulder. "Sorry, you're not Francisco."

"Francisco?" Rey turned to him, smiling. "No, he goes by Marco."

Busted. She'd blown his cover. And it was his own fault. He gripped her wrist, ready to run if the guy posed any danger.

The little man broke into a grin. "Are you Francisco Flores's brother? He used to tend bar here before he got hired at that new club downtown. I'm Antonio, the club manager. Come see me if you need anything." He was already moving to greet another patron.

Double busted. Rey yanked her wrist from his grasp. "You have a brother named Francisco?"

He nodded.

She narrowed her eyes. "He's the professional model, not you." It was a statement, not a question.

"That's right." He pulled her into an alcove near the coat check and spoke in a low, urgent tone. "I offered to take his place while he auditioned in L.A. for a soap opera. It was his big break, but his modeling agency wouldn't let him cancel his appointment with you."

Rey glared at him, her mouth pursed. It was so important for her to understand, to forgive his deception. He wanted to totally come clean with her, but he was already pushing his luck here in the club. He'd left his pistol behind and had only a switchblade hidden in his boot.

She sighed, her face relaxing into its customary beauty. "All right. I understand doing a favor for a brother. I knew something was wrong, but I thought you were getting back into modeling after taking a few years off."

"No, I've never modeled."

"I could tell." She raised an eyebrow. "So what do you do when you're not rescuing your brother?"

Rescuing the world, it felt like. "What I told you before. Import and export, international business."

"In Miami?"

"Yes." They needed to leave before Francisco's friend Antonio returned with any more questions. "I'll understand if you're upset with my deception and want to go home." He angled his body toward the exit.

"No, Marco, I forgive you." She finally smiled at him, her moist red lips parting invitingly. "Let's stay and dance."

Equal parts elation and desperation rushed through him. What if someone else recognized him?

"I'd be very disappointed if we left. And you'd be disappointed if you didn't get to see my dress." She finally opened the lapels of her cloak, unveiling herself.

Marco's tongue stuck to the roof of his mouth. She was a goddess. Her blond hair gleamed, twisted off her neck with a golden clasp. A golden halter dress fastened around her neck and skimmed over her plump breasts, tiny waist and voluptuous hips. Her nipples poked at the fabric like two Spanish doubloons.

"What do you think?" She twirled around and he groaned. A long, smooth expanse of back curved down to the tiny dimple at the base of her spine. If he hooked a finger inside the dress, he would touch the bare curve of her ass.

He yanked off his own leather jacket and grabbed hers. Tossing them at the coat-check attendant, he shoved the claim ticket into his rapidly tightening pants pocket. "Let's dance."

He guided her through the crush of people. Heads turned as they found a spot at the edge of the dance floor. She stood taller than the other women and most of the men, a golden beacon shining in the dark room.

Just as they reached the dance floor the band segued into a fast-tempoed song. She hesitated, obviously unsure of her next move.

"It's easy. All you have to do is move to the music." He put his hands on her hips and guided them back and forth.

"So salsa dancing is mostly shaking your ass," she shouted over the horn section.

"It's more complicated than that, but ass-shaking is a major part." Although the swing of her breasts under the tiny halter was also a big attraction.

He saw several men lurking nearby but ignored them. He knew he was rude in not letting any other men cut in on him and Rey. Salsa dancing was usually informal, with partners changing several times during an evening.

Rey leaned into him, her nipples pressing against his chest through the thin gold knit. "I think some of those men want to dance with me."

"Too bad." The band slipped into a slow number, the singer crooning about a lost love.

"What if I want to dance with them?" Her voice was teasing and husky.

"I don't want my woman to dance with anyone else."

"Am I your woman?" Her blue eyes were serious.

"You know you are." He swallowed hard. "Reina, I want to tell you something."

A younger man swaggered over to them and asked Reina to dance. By the time Marco sent him away with a blistering barrage of Cuban discouragement, the moment for confession had passed. He'd have to wait until they had more privacy.

Until then he'd take advantage of the sexy salsa rhythms. He brushed his fingers over the dimple at the base of her spine.

She leaned into him, her breath quickening. "Yes or no?"

"Yes or no what?"

"Have you decided if I'm wearing any underwear?"

His cock stiffened even more. "I'll need to investigate further."

Antonio appeared behind Rey, his expression urgent. Marco pulled his hand out of her dress and swung around.

"Two men were asking questions about you at the bar." Antonio spoke in rapid Spanish, guessing correctly that Rey wouldn't understand. "I didn't think they were your friends."

Marco whipped around to see whom Rodríguez had sent, but the crowd blocked his view of the bar. "You're right." Marco was already moving toward the nearest exit. "It's probably the lady's ex-boyfriend and his brother. When she broke up with him, he slapped her around."

Antonio spit out a foul Spanish curse. "Follow me." He made his way through the dancers.

Rey's eyes widened. "Marco, what's happening?"

He didn't know Antonio but had no choice but to trust him. "Antonio has someplace special to show us."

"*Sí,* very romantic," the club manager called over his shoulder. The band was muted as he led them through a door labeled Private and up a darkened flight of stairs.

Antonio flipped a switch, and small crystal wall lamps revealed a long hallway paneled in rich, dark wood. "Here we are." He stepped to a large panel and punched a code into a hidden keypad. A door swung open on silent hinges.

"A secret room." Rey looked from one man to another.

"I can rely on your discretion that no one learns about these rooms?"

Marco shook his hand, speaking quietly in Spanish. "I will not betray your kindness."

"*Bueno.* Give me half an hour to find these men and get rid of them." Antonio gestured at the narrow bar set along the side wall. "Please feel free to sample some beverages. No one will bother you here." He closed the door noiselessly behind him.

Marco walked over to the bar and found what he was looking for. He'd bet Rey had never tried a *mojito,* and he could use a drink, too. "Do you like limes?"

"Limes?" Rey turned to him with her hands on her hips. "Your friend whisks us off to some secret salsa-club Batcave and you ask me about limes?"

Uh-oh. She was royally pissed. "I have rum and cola if you'd prefer."

"I'd *prefer* that you tell me the truth, Marco Francisco Flores-or-maybe-not-Flores."

"Actually my full name is Marco Santiago Flores."

"Well, Marco Santiago, why don't you tell me what the hell is going on?"

"Look, that had to be Flores's brother dancing with the blonde with the juicy ass." Chucho licked his lips. "Man, when we find him, I want an hour alone with her."

His brother scoffed. "An hour? You'd only need three minutes."

"If you're lonely, Nico, we should find a goat for you."

Nico muttered an epithet and craned his neck. "Holy shit, he looks a lot like Flores. But *el jefe* says to do nothing. Just find where he's staying."

"Nothing?" Chucho sulked, caressing the switch-blade in his pocket. "I want to cut that golden dress off her."

"Stop playing pocket pool and pay attention." Nico grabbed his brother's ear and twisted as he lost sight of their target.

"Ay! Let go!" Chucho rubbed his ear. "We can't miss them if we stand by the bar. They'll get thirsty soon."

A new voice came from behind them. "Looking for someone?" asked a short man in a fancy suit.

Chucho sneered. "Beat it, Tiny."

"Oh, I'm not Tiny." Two huge bouncers had come up behind the man. "This is Tiny." He gestured to one bouncer. Tiny had thighs as big as the trunks of palm trees and biceps the size of coconuts. A thick scar cut through his black brow, and his shaved scalp gleamed pink in the spotlights from the stage.

"And this is Sammy." The bouncer on the right cracked a feral smile, its white gleam bisecting the dark skin of his cheeks. A diamond-encrusted tooth winked in the dim light.

Chucho and Nico stepped back, only to find the wall behind them.

"Now that you know our names, maybe you can tell us yours." The short man's eyes glittered ominously. "We can all be friends. Tiny and Sammy love to make new friends." The bouncers grinned and cracked their knuckles.

The brothers glanced at each other: what now?

"I'M WAITING FOR THAT explanation." Rey crossed her arms and fumed as Marco took his own sweet time crushing leaves and adding rum and other liquids.

He finally set two drinks on the granite bar top. "Let's dance." Marco walked to an intercom system in the wall and twisted a dial. A set of hidden speakers piped in the salsa band's throbbing rhythms.

"Marco." She had to almost shout over the music. "Marco, I don't really want to dance."

He shook his head and dragged her close. Instead of swinging her into the complex rhythmic patterns she'd observed downstairs, he wrapped his arms around her and put his mouth next to her ear. "Reina, I need to tell you something, but it's not safe here."

She tried to pull away to stare at him, but he held her in an iron grip. "Not safe?" Her throat went dry. "Why aren't we leaving right now? Or calling the cops?"

He shook his head. "I swear, I'll tell you as soon as I can. There were two men downstairs who want to find me. We'll leave as soon as Antonio gets rid of them."

"Gets rid of them? Like 'sleeping with the fishes' gets rid of them?"

He finally let her go. "Gets his bouncers to throw them out, that's all."

"Are you in trouble with the law?"

"No, not at all." He looked faintly amused and picked up his drink.

"Any alcohol or drug problems?" She really hoped not. They'd been careful with protection, but the thought of him abusing that wonderful body made her skin crawl.

He choked midsip. He looked at the drink in his hand and set it down. "I've spent every single day and almost every night with you for the past two weeks. Have I ever been drunk?"

She shook her head. A couple beers or a glass of wine was the most she'd seen him drink. "And drugs?" she pressed.

He grabbed her hand and clasped it against his heart. "I swear on the soul of my father. Drugs are filthy poison and the creatures who sell them are animals."

Rey studied him. As far as she could see, he was telling the truth about drugs. And he'd almost laughed at the idea of being a criminal. "All right, I do believe you, but you're still not off the hook."

"I understand. But come try your cocktail. It's a *mojito,* Miami's answer to the mint julep. It's not as good as when you pick the limes fresh off the trees, but you still get a taste of Miami."

Rey sipped from the icy glass. Sweet mint bubbled over her tongue, balanced by the tang of the half lime floating in the goblet. "It's very good." She drained her glass and held it out for a refill.

Marco laughed. "Are you sure you want another right now? There's a lot of rum in there."

"Swedish Christmas punch is hard liquor mixed with red wine."

He poured a fresh glass for her. "If you can handle that, my little *mojito* is like a soft drink." He sipped from his own glass.

Rey leaned her hips against the leather-topped table. Despite her alcohol tolerance, she hadn't eaten since lunch. She drank half of her *mojito* and held the icy glass against her burning cheek.

"Are you all right, Reina?" Marco set down his drink and moved closer to her.

"Just a little hot, I think." The little room was close and stuffy.

"You're blazing hot, *querida*." His eyes darkened to tawny brown.

"I need to cool off." She mischievously ran the glass over her other cheek and down her bare neck. A drop of condensation ran into the hollow between her breasts. "Ah, that's better."

"Do you know what's better?" He bent to lick the droplet off her skin.

She clutched the slippery glass. "That didn't cool me off." Her plan of teasing him was backfiring.

"How about this?" He pulled the *mojito* from her nerveless fingers and circled the icy glass around the thrumming pulse at the base of her neck.

He traced a finger under the edge of her halter, pausing at the top swell of her breast. Its peak immediately tightened and she shivered.

"Are you sure you're not cooled off yet?" He stared where her nipples strained against the thin gold knit. "You seem a bit chilled."

"I'm fine." She was losing control of the situation and stumbled against the table. He scooped her up with one muscular arm and sat her on the tabletop. She braced her palms behind her and automatically widened her thighs for balance. He stepped between them, wedging his pelvis against hers.

He pressed the *mojito* glass against her nipple. She gasped his name as the cold traveled through the fabric. Before she caught her breath, he pressed it against the other.

"You like that?" he whispered.

Rey couldn't answer for a second, still shuddering from the icy sensation and the rasp of his erection on the tender sliver of skin above her stockings. She was off balance, both physically and emotionally. "Yes."

"You'll like this even better." He reached up to the nape of her neck and unfastened the hooks holding her top closed.

Her breasts sprang free as he dragged the gold knit down to her waist. With her hands behind her, her breasts thrust up, aching nipples tilted toward Marco's mouth.

He rubbed the glass over one pale pink tip. Icy-hot sensations shot to her throbbing clit. She jerked her hips forward, pulsing against his erection. He repeated it again on her other breast, leaving her shivering from cold and desire. "Marco, we can't do this here. Anyone might come in." She fumbled with the straps to her halter.

"The only man coming in is *me*." He swirled a finger across the damp pink tip.

"Oh, you think so?" She gave up trying to fasten the tiny hooks at the back of her neck and held the fabric against her.

"I know so. Antonio told me no one else knows the key code to this room. And he turned off the fiber-optic surveillance cameras and microphones for us."

"This room is bugged?" Rey looked around in shock.

"Of course." He looked amused. "The club owner holds highly sensitive business meetings here."

"What kind of business?"

He grinned. "Do you really want to know?"

How *did* Marco know these people? He saw the skeptical look on her face and stepped closer. "Would you like the rest of your *mojito?*"

"No, you can finish it." She wanted a clear head to decide what to do.

He took a drink and swirled it around his mouth. Tugging her top loose, he fastened his chilly lips on her nipple, sucking and tugging until her greedy flesh filled his mouth. She wove her fingers through his hair as he pinched her other straining peak.

He stepped back, leaving her dangling half-naked off the table. She sat up and pressed her knees together to soothe the ache between her legs.

He sipped his drink and traced his fingers over her knee. "You never did tell me if you were wearing any panties."

"Why don't you find out?" She inched her thighs apart, encouraging him to explore her aching sex.

He obliged, running a finger around the wide lace band of her stocking. "Your skin is like silk." He slid his finger higher until he reached her damp curls. "You're naughty, not even wearing a thong. What if your skirt crept up when we were dancing? Anyone could see your creamy thighs and your golden triangle." He tugged gently on her hair.

She shuddered as he glided along the seam of her sex. "It was too dark to see anything."

"Every man in the club was staring at you." His finger circled the damp bud and lifted. "Did it make you hot to know that?"

"No, Marco." She wiggled closer, her breath coming in quick pants. "I only want you."

"Good." He sheathed two fingers in her, her hidden muscles convulsing around him. She thrust her hips forward until her clit bumped the pad of his thumb.

He caressed her, sending shock waves spiraling from her womb. She curled her fingers over the table's edge, her nails digging into the varnished wood. Just as her orgasm began to pulse, he pulled out.

"Marco!" She almost screamed in frustration.

"What, *querida?*" He took another sip from the *mojito,* which he hadn't put down since he'd started caressing her. He was cool and collected, while she had melted into a puddle on the table.

"If you don't touch me now, I'll have to touch myself." She unhooked one hand from the table and caressed the sliver of skin above her stocking, moving closer and closer to the pulsing nub crowning her thighs.

"Go ahead." His tone was even, but his eyes glittered in the dim light. His cock pressed long and thick against the tight placket of his pants.

She marveled at his iron control. Maybe she could break it. "Sit in that chair."

He refilled his glass and relaxed into the heavy leather armchair.

She stood, the stiletto heels of her golden sandals teetering in the plush carpet. She wiggled her dress over her hips, peeking at him over her bare shoulder. Stepping out of the golden pool of fabric at her feet, she hopped onto the table, naked except for her stockings and sandals. "So you like to watch?" She spread her legs wide, the brass tacks on the table pressing into the soft flesh of her bottom.

"Sometimes."

She was gratified to hear his voice rasp. "Tell me what you want me to do." She was suddenly nervous. She had touched herself briefly before their sauna session but had never given herself an orgasm in front of any man before.

"Lick your fingers."

She inserted two fingers between her lips, drawing them deep. She circled her tongue around them, their thickness and length reminding her of his cock. "Do you remember when I sucked on you in the sauna?"

"Yes." His voice was calm, but she saw his knuckles whiten as he gripped the arms of the chair.

She pinched her nipple with her damp fingers and trailed her hand slowly down her body, pausing just above the nest of golden hair.

His eyes dilated almost to black. "Touch your clit."

She paused for a second, tracing wet patterns around her belly button.

"Do it now, Reina." He was a man pushed to the brink of his control. His hand had strayed to the front of his pants, stroking his erection. "Or else I'm going to make myself come and you won't get my cock inside you."

The threat was enough to make her obey. She gasped as she explored the knot of nerves nestled in her slick, swollen folds. Faster and faster she circled her throbbing clitoris, her head lolling.

"Suck on your other fingers and touch your tits." His crude language aroused her even further, spurring her imagination to new sensual heights.

Instead of sucking on her fingers, she cupped a breast in her palm and dipped her head. She took a deep breath and darted her tongue out to lick her own nipple, jumping slightly at the double sensation.

She heard a thud and looked up, startled. Marco had dropped his *mojito,* droplets splashing onto his slacks.

"Do that again." His voice was hoarse. The glass rolled under his chair as he gripped the armrests.

"This?" Emboldened by his response, she let her tongue swirl around the sensitive areola. It felt really sexy, especially when he made little groaning noises and shifted in the chair.

She sped up the caresses between her thighs, enjoying her power over him without even touching him. He murmured Spanish endearments to her. When she couldn't stand the exquisite pressure anymore, she closed her eyes and let the memory of his burning golden gaze carry her to the peak of a blazing climax.

"You are the sexiest woman I've ever known." Rey's smooth body sprawled decadently on the table, the golden lips of her lush pink sex spread wide open. Moisture trickled, pooling on the leather tabletop. He stood and yanked open his belt, sighing with relief as his aching cock sprang upward.

She looked at him through slumberous blue eyes. "Come here."

He was already only a step away from her. He lifted her boneless body and balanced her on the sandals' tiny heels. "Turn around."

She rested her ass on the table. "I have something you need."

"I know you do, baby." He dipped his fingers into her melting flesh, her vagina pulsing with orgasmic aftershocks.

"Wait," she panted, reaching under the band of her stocking. "This." She pulled out a hidden condom.

"You planned to fuck me here, didn't you?" He swelled even longer, a drop of moisture beading on the end of his cock. "Did you want me to take you in the bathroom and push deep inside you?" He moved his finger faster, her juices trickling onto his hand.

She nodded frantically, pushing her tight, hot body up and down his fingers.

"Or did you want to dance to a dark corner of the floor and get my cock inside you in front of everyone?"

Her knees weakened and he caught her around the waist.

"Turn around and spread your legs. Put your palms on the table."

She widened her stance and sent a coy look over her shoulder. Her long, smooth back sparkled with tiny gold flecks in the intimate light, dipping in to her tiny waist and swelling into the luscious velvety halves of her bottom. Cuban women had nothing on Rey's booty, he decided.

"Are you arresting me, Officer Flores?" She widened her eyes in mock surprise.

If only he could tell her how close to the truth she was. "You're under arrest for speeding."

"Speeding?" She leaned forward from the waist and pressed her full breasts against the tabletop, gasping as her nipples rubbed the leather.

"You made yourself come much too fast. As an officer of the law, I have an obligation to slow you down."

"I'm sorry, Officer. It's been so long since a man came inside me." She was really getting into their sexual role-play.

"I'm going to have to frisk you, ma'am." He moved behind her and palmed her breasts. She moaned and arched into him. "I got a report that you trapped a man between your tits and wouldn't let him go."

"Is he filing a complaint?" She gasped as he pinched her swollen nipples, still slick from where she had licked herself.

"His only complaint is that you haven't done it again." He released her breasts and skimmed past her rib cage to outside of her legs. He knelt and cupped her slender foot still encased in the sexy gold sandal. He slid his hands slowly up her leg, caressing her toned calf and firm thigh. He stopped at the band of skin above the stocking, his fingers teasing the warm, wet cleft between her legs. She tried to grind on him, but he moved his hands to her other leg and repeated the tantalizingly sensuous frisk.

"Marco, I need you!"

"There's one place I haven't checked yet." He realized he still had the condom in his hand and ripped the packet open with his teeth. He smoothed it over his cock. The latex was still warm from her skin and it clung tightly to him. He almost climaxed as he pushed inside her, watching his shaft disappear between her plump buttocks and fill her pink sex. Gritting his teeth, he managed to say, "How long has it been?"

"Forever." She tossed her glorious hair over her shoulders and pressed her palms against the tabletop.

"How long?" He pulled out of her.

"Marco!"

"That's Officer Flores to you." He nudged her opening with his tip. "Before we met, how long since a man's cock had been inside you?"

She wiggled backward, but he denied her. "Seven months," she admitted.

He immediately rewarded her with his shaft. "See? An easy question."

"How long for you?" She moaned as he stopped moving inside her tight warmth.

"I'm the one asking the questions." He leaned forward, his mouth only millimeters from her ear. "Have you ever let a man bend you over a table and fuck you?" He pulled out.

"No!" she moaned.

He pushed inside and withdrew, gritting his teeth as her tiny muscles threatened to squeeze him dry. "Did you ever kneel and press your tits together for another man's cock?"

"No!" She was half sobbing with frustration, her hips tilting against him. "Oh, God, Marco, I can't stand it!"

"I'll let you get off with a warning." He pounded inside her as sweat popped out on his brow and his balls pulled tight against his body. "This is for no one else, Rey. Just me." His breath was ragged and fierce.

"Only you, Marco." She muffled a scream as he reached around her luscious thigh and strummed her pulsing clit.

"Only you, Reina. Forever." It was the first time he'd promised forever to a woman, but it was right and perfect.

"Forever," she echoed on a breathy sigh. Then neither said anything as he increased his pace.

Her tight sheath contracted along his length. He circled her clit once more and pinched her nipples. She bucked against him and sobbed his name, her orgasm squeezing him until he came with a loud groan, pouring out his seed and his soul.

"*DIOS MÍO,* YOU SMELL." Chucho folded the switchblade and stuffed it in his pocket.

Nico tossed the cut yellow nylon rope on the ground. "You don't exactly smell like orange blossoms, either, *hermano.*"

His younger brother brushed shredded lime peel off his pants. "We're lucky those bouncers just tied us together and tossed us in the Dumpster."

"*Sí,* they must not work for the boss," Nico said, not even wanting to mention his name aloud. "His man inside DEA was just found in the Everglades with an extra smile in his neck."

"Who was that guy anyway?"

"A computer analyst with a bad habit." Nico lifted his empty pinky finger to his nose and made a sniffing motion. "He tracked Flores to Chicago in exchange for what? His own death."

Chucho nodded, for once agreeing with him. "Maybe that blonde belongs to the short guy. He kept telling me to stay away from her." Chucho grabbed his ribs where Tiny had kicked him several times.

"So why was she shaking her booty with the brother?" Nico blinked, trying to see out of his rapidly swelling eye.

"The short guy probably has a dick to match. Too bad she can't get a load of mine." Chucho's boast would have been more impressive if he hadn't had a pink tropical drink umbrella stuck to his shoulder.

"Forget her. Let's get out of this damn alley and find Flores's brother." Nico strode off, cursing as his boot heel skidded on a banana peel. "The club's closing. I'll watch the side exit and you go to the front."

Chucho sneered. "He's probably been tucked in bed for hours with that blonde." He made a grinding motion with his hips.

"Get going!" Nico stared at the side exit, not really expecting to see anyone. The man had probably ducked out the back door as soon as he was spotted.

Minutes passed. Even the musicians had left. Finally the club lights winked off. Nico gave up and went to find his brother.

"Any luck?"

Chucho shook his head. "No. So what do we do now?"

Nico thought hard. "If they took a cab home, maybe we can trace them through the cab companies. That blonde will be hard to miss."

Chucho groaned. "You know how many cabs were around here? Especially if they caught one a few blocks over?"

Nico slugged his brother in the shoulder. "If you wanna tell the boss we lost him in a salsa club, don't expect to live too long. A man like that is a shark, and you and I are just the bloody chum."

16

MARCO BOLTED UPRIGHT IN bed and snatched his pistol off the nightstand. His heart pounded and his mouth was as dry as if he'd been bobbing on the ocean again.

"Marco, what is it?" Rey's warm arm came around his waist. She'd fallen asleep in the cab, exhausted by anxiety and several cocktails on an empty stomach.

"I'm all right." He'd fallen asleep after he'd tucked her in, leaving his pistol within easy reach. He shoved the gun under his pillow just before she turned on a small bedside lamp. The sheets were a twisted mess binding his legs together. "Just a bad dream."

He wasn't surprised that he'd dreamed about the raft. Those nightmares always crept up from the dregs of his past when he was under enormous stress.

Rey uncurled herself from the linens, her long hair glowing gold over her creamy breasts. She slipped off the bed and walked naked across the floor. He straightened, pleasantly distracted by the sway of her bottom.

She returned from the bathroom with a water glass. "Drink this. You'll feel better."

He was already feeling better seeing her stand in front of him.

"I think we need to talk." She shrugged into her pink silk robe and knotted the belt around her slender waist.

Hell, no, he didn't want to talk, but she deserved an explanation after he'd dragged her into his mess. "First let me tell you about how I came to the U.S. It's all kind of tied in to what happened tonight."

"You did tell me that. You and your family left Cuba on a terrible little raft and floated to Florida. I can't even imagine how it must have been."

"It was even worse than I told you." He took a deep breath. "My father was a poet and an intellectual. Neither of those kinds of men is welcome in a totalitarian society."

He felt Rey's intent stare but didn't look at her. It was easier to get through his story if he didn't see what had to be sympathy in her eyes. "My father disguised his political protests in poetry and gained popular support. Our last name, Flores, means 'flowers.' Average Cubans who never dared defy the government wore white flowers in their lapels." He shrugged. "His writings also attracted attention from the wrong people."

Rey touched his arm. "What happened?" Her voice was low and sorrowful. She obviously knew what was coming next.

"He was fired from the university as unsuitable for the formation of young Cuban minds." Marco laughed bitterly. "That was a gross understatement. The administration was too stupid to realize that he'd taught the literature of dissent for years. Rousseau, Thoreau, Thomas Paine. Our *mamá* was so proud of him. She knew the dangers but never asked him to deny his belief in a free Cuba."

"Your mother sounds like an amazing woman. It must have broken her heart to see him go into danger."

"*Papi* read his poetry at a pro-democracy rally. Police spies arrested my father and took him to the political prison on the Isle of Youth. He died from pneumonia a couple months later. We never saw him again."

Rey bit her lower lip to stop its trembling. Marco pulled her into his arms. "Hey, don't cry. I made my peace with it a long time ago."

"Are you sure?" She rubbed her warm hands along his back. He relaxed slightly into her touch, some anger dissipating.

"*Papi* may have been a university professor, but he wasn't naive. When he read that poem, he knew he'd wind up in prison or dead. After his arrest, crushed flowers were mysteriously strewn on the streets. His poem is still read at anti-Castro rallies all over Florida."

"So your mother escaped to Miami with you."

"Yeah, we were the lucky ones. The Coast Guard found us before we died of dehydration."

"Oh, sweetheart." She pressed her fist against her mouth. "But what can that possibly have to do with those men in the club?"

Marco sighed. Now came the difficult part of his story. His eyes were gritty and burning, and he had to piss. "Let me go splash some water on my face. I promise I'll tell you everything then."

Rey studied his tired face and nodded. "All right, but don't plan on sneaking out on me. That bathroom doesn't even have a window."

He gave her a weak grin and ran his fingers through his tangled curls. "I don't have to leave you yet."

His response made her shiver inside at the thought of letting him go. He trudged into the bathroom and shut the door.

She needed to keep busy while she waited. The bed linens were a mess, the sheets pulled loose and the goose-down duvet half on the floor. She tucked the sheets in and straightened the duvet.

Marco's pillow was sweaty and twisted from his bad dream. She picked it up for a good fluffing.

"Rey, no!"

Puzzled, she looked up and saw Marco sprinting naked from the bathroom, his feet skidding on one of her area rugs.

"What?" She looked at the bed and saw the weapon. "Oh, my God!" She stumbled, pulling the sheet with her. The gun fell onto the floor and they both cringed.

He snatched it up, checking it expertly.

"At least it's not loaded, right?" She pushed her hair away from her face. "That's why it didn't go off."

"It's loaded." He should have looked ridiculous standing there naked with a gun, but the grim expression on his face drove away her incipient fit of hysterical giggles. "The reason it didn't go off is the safety was on."

"A loaded gun? You brought a loaded gun into my home? Into my bed?" She clutched the robe against her, a chill penetrating into her bones that had nothing to do with the room's temperature.

He quirked an ironic smile. "A gun's no good if it's unloaded, Reina. What am I supposed to do, throw it at someone?"

"Why do you even need a gun, Marco?" She froze.

"This is because of those men at the club, isn't it? What do they want with you?"

"*Querida,* they want me dead."

17

"DEAD?" THE BLOOD DRAINED from Rey's face, leaving her naturally pale skin a sickly greenish color. "Those men want to kill you?"

Marco realized he was still naked and brandishing his gun. Careful not to spook her, he tucked the pistol into the nightstand's top drawer and put on his robe. "Reina." He sat on the bed and tugged her next to him. She flinched away.

He tried again, taking her cold hand in his. He searched carefully for the right words. If he couldn't get her to understand, she would never trust him again. Without her trust, they had nothing. And without her he *was* nothing, he realized with a shock. "I left Miami on the run almost three weeks ago."

"It's about drugs, isn't it?" She shot to her feet, pointing a shaking finger at him.

"Yes, but it's not what you think."

"Oh, Marco, how could you? You swore to me you weren't involved in drugs." Tears spilled down her anguished face. She turned her back to him and hunched over.

"Listen to me, Rey." He grabbed her shoulders and turned her to face him.

"No!" She struggled in his arms. "Get out! Get your things and leave before I call the cops!"

He released her, not wanting to hurt her. "No need to call the cops. I *am* a cop."

"A cop?" The perfect bow of her upper lip twisted into a sneer. "Why would a cop model in the nude? Won't that get you into trouble at the station house?"

"Reina, please." This was turning into his worst nightmare, and all of his own doing. "I'm not in local law enforcement. I'm a sworn agent of the United States Drug Enforcement Agency."

She laughed. "A fed. I think I saw this episode before on *Miami Vice* reruns. Where are your white sports coat and sockless loafers?"

"I had to wear expensive Italian suits with hand-tooled leather shoes. The short guys wore cowboy boots with four-inch heels."

She narrowed her eyes. "Let's say all of this is true. What are you doing in Chicago modeling nude for me?"

"Having the time of my life."

"Marco, I'm serious," she chided.

"I am, too." He tried to gather her in his arms, but she neatly sidestepped him. He heaved a sigh and continued. "I volunteered to infiltrate a Cuban-based drug smuggling operation because I was native-born, knew the island and had the right accent. After a year of undercover work, we had enough evidence to go to trial. If I can't testify next week, the charges will be reduced or dismissed."

"Can't you show me a badge or something to prove who you are?"

He was already shaking his head. "I left all of my IDs

in Miami. I couldn't risk calling attention to myself in the metal detectors at airport security with a DEA badge."

"But you smuggled a gun through?"

"I bought it here from a gun dealer who wasn't picky about ID or registration."

"Don't you know it's illegal to own a handgun in Chicago?"

He laughed. "Getting caught with a pistol is the least of my concerns. The only reason I came to Chicago was to get my brother Francisco to safety, somewhere where it would be harder to find him. I came prepared to convince, bribe or kidnap him to get out of town, but the only way he left was when I promised to take his place with you."

"And your mother is on her honeymoon." She thought for a minute. "About your father and sailing over on a raft. That wasn't just a story, was it?" Her eyes were pleading with him.

He clenched his hands. "God, no. It's the reason I took the assignment. Look, come sit here next to me."

She hesitated, fussing with the lapels of her robe. "I don't know, Marco. This sounds very far-fetched."

"We only met a few weeks ago, but you know me, Reina."

She stopped fiddling with the knot at her waist and stared at him. *Did* she know him? His hawklike hazel eyes watched her guardedly. He'd never shown any intent to harm her. In fact, he even roughed up Stefan a bit for her. But did that make him a thug or a cop?

"Oh, all right." She plopped down beside him on the bed. "Start from the beginning."

"I didn't tell you everything about our raft trip. My mother paid a man called *El Lobo,* the wolf, to take us to Miami on his raft. Once we were at sea, he made advances to my mother." He swallowed hard. "That man sliced Francisco's leg bloody and threatened to throw him to the sharks if *Mamá* didn't do what he wanted. I tried to fight him, but he punched me in the face and knocked me cold for a few minutes."

"Your poor mother." Rey bit her lip, remembering how scared she had been at first when Stefan had threatened her in the Art Institute. "All alone on the ocean with no one to come to her rescue."

"No one but me, a skinny twelve-year-old. I staggered to my feet. He was kissing and groping my mother while my brother whimpered. I bashed him in the head with an oar. We tied him up with duct tape we'd used for patching the raft." His hands made fists on his thighs.

She grabbed his left hand. He turned to look at her, his eyes dark with old memories. "You saved her, Marco."

"No. She saved us, my brother and me. She was willing to do anything to keep us alive. And now I repay her by getting twisted up in *El Lobo*'s sick machinations." He managed a dry laugh. "If he doesn't get me, my mother will. I can just hear her now. 'I didn't take you out of Cuba for you to go back there and get into trouble.'"

"Your mother supported your father when he confronted evil, and she'll support you, too."

Marco stared straight ahead, lost in his memories. "That man *is* pure evil. I saw it in his eyes when I was just a child and saw it again years later. He regained consciousness right before the Coast Guard found us. The hate shining from his yellow eyes was chilling. He was deported to Cuba, years later emerging as the head of a Caribbean drug-smuggling ring. He's got connections to the Colombian cartels. His real name is Juan Carlos Rodríguez, and he's the man I have to testify against."

Her hand flew to her mouth. "Oh, my God. How did he even learn about your investigation?"

He shook his head. "Over a year's work, thirteen months living with those *animales,* thinking like them… one day it all fell apart. We had all the evidence we needed, but we got greedy and wanted a little more just to make sure Rodríguez would never see the light of day again.

"Except my cover got blown. He'd paid enough drugs or money to someone at DEA to find out who I really was. And with his money, with his connections, it didn't take long before he found my mother and my brother."

He clutched her hand, his words coming out painfully. "Reina, what have I done? To fight crime I became like a criminal. For what? Vengeance? When my family discovers what I did, I will lose their trust. Just like I have lost yours."

"And this whole story is true." It was a statement more than a question. "Hiding at the salsa club, you carrying this gun. You really are a federal agent."

"I swear on the soul of my father." He clasped her hand to his heart.

As soon as he said that, a weight lifted off her. "Since we're revealing our deepest secrets, I guess I'll have to reciprocate."

He watched her warily, his fingers tight around hers.

She took a deep breath. "Even before you told me the truth I fell in love with you." She'd never told any man that before, not even in her infatuated youth.

"Do you—" He stopped to clear his throat. "Do you still feel the same way?" His gaze was molten gold, burning her until heat pooled between her thighs.

"Of course." She slipped her hand inside the deep V of his robe, his heart pounding under her fingertips.

"Oh, thank God." He swept her into his arms, murmuring long, sexy streams of Spanish as he feathered kisses on her closed eyelids, cheeks and jaw. She relaxed into his embrace, kissing him eagerly before shoving him away.

"Whatever you told me sounded very pretty, but I didn't understand a word. If you have something you want me to know, tell me in English." Her stomach clenched in nervous anticipation.

"I was speaking Spanish?" He laughed. "I always do when I'm excited."

"So?" she demanded.

"What I was saying is that I'll love you forever and never want to be without you." He lifted her off his lap and went down on one knee in front of her. Rey covered her gasp with her fist.

His face was serious as he took her hand. "Until I take the witness stand, I'm not free to ask you for anything, Reina."

"What do you mean?"

"If something happens to me, I don't want to leave you behind to grieve."

"You stupid man." She shoved him with her free hand, toppling him onto his ass.

"If you want me naked, all you have to do is ask," he joked, adjusting his robe where it had flown open, revealing his thighs and crotch.

"Do you think I wouldn't grieve for you, cry for you, miss you forever just because you won't ask me for a commitment?" She was gulping in deep breaths, trying to keep from screaming her pain and frustration.

He sat next to her on the chaise. "Not just a commitment. Marriage."

"Marriage?" She gaped at him. The M-word hadn't even crept across her subconscious, but now it was the perfect idea. "But you can't ask me now?" She was dying to say yes.

"Reina, please." He placed his hand over hers. "A man does not make commitments and put himself into danger."

"Like your father?"

He sighed and twined his fingers between hers. "Yes. He did the right thing but at a terrible cost to all of us. I won't do that to you."

She smoothed her palm over his tight jaw, the tiny black hairs tickling her. "I understand. I'm willing to wait as long as I know what's in your heart." She feathered kisses across his cheek.

He captured her mouth with his and pulled her onto the soft pillows. He opened the silken lapels of her robe so his hands covered her breasts.

She was just as eager, shoving his robe off his shoulders. He tossed the heavy terry cloth away, diving onto her.

"I promise, I'll return to you." He nudged her knees apart and rubbed his hair-roughened thigh against the swollen folds of her sex, his penis fitting into the groove where her leg met her hip.

"I want you inside me." She twisted against him, wanting more, wanting him to fill her.

"I can't," he rasped, a bead of sweat trailing down his temple. "I used the last condom in the box."

She drew in a shaky breath. "Without one."

His pupils dilated until only a narrow amber rim showed. "I shouldn't, but…" He moaned as she cupped his penis and rubbed the bare head against her clit, the silver bead at the tip mingling with her own juices. She grew bolder and shifted her hips so his hot, pulsing flesh teased at the entrance to her wet passage. "Oh, God, that's so good." He jerked against her, almost slipping inside.

She'd never even considered making love without protection before, but she trusted Marco. "I'm healthy and on the Pill."

"I had a full physical and blood tests before I went into protective custody. Everything came back clean."

"Do it. Give me your bare cock inside me."

He succumbed to her enticement and slid into her with a gasp. He was scorching hot inside her. The thick ridge around the head of his penis rubbed every inch of her as he moved in and withdrew slowly. The satiny skin of his shaft stretched her until she spasmed around him, a mini orgasm that only gave her a tiny taste of what he would do to her.

Marco gritted his teeth. "You feel so good, I can hardly stand it." Her wet, hot vagina clenched around him. Making love with his beautiful Reina was always incredible, but this was phenomenal.

He rocked against her as she clutched his shoulders and wrapped her long, strong legs around his waist, pulling him deeper until his cock was buried to the hilt.

The pink robe framed her breasts like a work of art, the color matching her tight nipples. He sucked on one perfect peak as it elongated and swelled under his tongue. He ran his tongue around the rim of her areola, almost coming at the memory of her licking her own nipples.

Since he wasn't ready to give up the mind-blowing pleasure of his bare flesh inside hers, he released her breast, admiring how rosy-red and engorged the tip had turned. Rey made little mewling sounds, tossing her golden hair and caressing his butt. He bent to the other breast, giving it the same loving attention until she surprised him.

He threw his head back as her cool fingers stroked and squeezed his balls.

"More," she whispered huskily. "Move inside me." He obliged and reached between them, flicking her clit until she moaned. He increased the pace of his thrusts, her tight, wet sheath squeezing his penis from head to base.

He knew he couldn't last much longer, was surprised he'd lasted as long as he had. All the while she cupped his balls, rubbing the rough flesh behind them as she matched his rhythm, grinding her hips into his.

She stiffened against him, her heels digging into his calves. "Oh, Marco, I'm coming." Her words trailed off in a gasp as her inner muscles tightened on him, an erotic flush creeping up her breasts. Her fingers tightened almost painfully on his sac as she came, sending him over the edge with her. He slammed into her, his hot seed bursting free for the first time in his life to mingle with her own juices and lubricate his frantic thrusts.

He finally slowed to a stop but stayed inside her for long minutes, not ever wanting to leave.

Rey lay in his embrace, his heart beating against hers. "That was amazing."

"I never knew it could be that way." He rolled over and cradled her head on his shoulders. "Someday we'll make love without any kind of protection."

"We just did." She twirled his chest hair around her fingers, glad he hadn't taken her silly suggestion to shave it off.

"Without *any* protection," he emphasized, "for me or for you."

"Oh." She looked up into his loving gaze and he nodded.

"I want to take you to Miami to meet my mother, play Cuban cabana boy on her pool furniture and ask you to marry me."

A tear spilled down her cheek. She wanted to hear the words so badly but knew he wouldn't propose until he was sure the danger was over. Fear clenched her stomach. "But it's not safe for you here. Those men might be able to find you."

"We gave them the slip at the club, thanks to Antonio. Everything's okay for a little while longer." He tried tickling her sides, but she smacked his hand away.

"Don't try to distract me!" She dashed away her tears with the back of her hand. "You need to leave Chicago right away. Put some distance between you and this man Rodríguez until you have to testify."

"I am leaving Chicago." His expression was grim.

"When?" A band of pain tightened in her chest. She sat up and swung her legs over the side of the bed. She knew it was safer for him, but it would kill her to see him go.

He moved behind her and wrapped his arms around her, his warmth unable to dispel the chill that had settled into her bones. "As soon as I make arrangements for a car. I need something inconspicuous and untraceable."

Rey figured he meant a stolen car. Under normal circumstances she would have disapproved, but now she would hot-wire a car herself if it would make him safe. "Promise me you'll tell me before you go."

His body tensed. She turned and gave him a hard stare. "Promise me you won't leave without telling me."

"No." He shook his head. "I'd be lying to you if I promised that, and I don't want to lie to you anymore."

"Marco!" Her frustration bubbled over. "You just can't leave me to wonder if you stepped out for a newspaper or if you had to go on the run again."

"Reina…" His arms tightened around her, almost squeezing the breath out of her. "It's killing me to have to leave you."

She heaved a shuddering sigh, knowing he might be killed if he stayed. They sat together on the edge of her bed for several silent minutes, not wanting to let go of each other.

He finally broke the quiet anguish surrounding them. "I'll give you my friend's cell phone number. If something happens, call him."

"All right." She nodded, eager for any scrap of information.

"If you do need to call him, try to use a pay phone. If you can't get to one, block the caller ID before dialing his number. And when he answers, ask for Lalo." He clasped her hand tight and stared intently at her. "You need to remember that so he knows I sent you. *Lalo.*"

"His name is Lalo?" That name was unfamiliar. "Does he speak English?"

Marco finally cracked a smile. "Somewhat. He's a cowboy from Texas."

She laughed at his small joke more than it deserved, trying not to cry again.

"Don't worry, *mi amor.* Soon we'll have a wonderful, happy home, maybe with a handsome little boy with black hair and blue eyes and a beautiful little girl with golden hair and golden eyes." He stroked her hair and kissed her brow gently.

Rey swallowed hard past the lump in her throat. She wanted that ideal life he described. But would facing that drug dealer cost him his own life?

JUAN CARLOS RODRÍGUEZ sat smoking his cigar and looking at the blue waters of Biscayne Bay. His yacht lay at anchor nearby, ready for whenever her master cared to sail away. The luxury vessel was a far cry from the first boat he'd sailed to America. Losing his raft and his freedom twenty years ago had made him appreciate the fine things he owned now. Things that would be seized by the American government if he did not kill Flores.

Gabriel knocked on his office door and entered without waiting for permission, an unusual breach. "What is it?" He set his cigar in the gold ashtray. "What is it?"

His assistant's narrow face was uncharacteristically flushed with excitement. "*Señor,* the García brothers have found Marco Flores in Chicago."

"Those two clowns found *him?* Not his brother?" If they sent him on a wild-goose chase, it would be the last thing they ever did.

"They spotted Flores in a dance club. He and his date left in a cab, and we happened to have connections to the cab company. The driver was happy to tell us their destination." Gabriel handed him the address and a map printed from the Internet.

"How do you know it is Flores and not his brother?"

"The brother has been auditioning for a Spanish soap opera in L.A. for the past three weeks. He got cast as the lead and the production company posted a press release as well as his photo on their Web site. There's no way the brother was in Chicago at that dance club." His assistant's eager demeanor reminded him of a puppy that had just brought a stick to its master.

"*Muy bien,* Gabriel." Rodríguez allowed himself a rare smile of approval. "Make travel arrangements for me to fly to Chicago."

"*Señor,* if the court finds out you have left Florida…"

Rodríguez cut him off with an impatient wave. "Do it!"

"*Sí, señor.*" Gabriel nodded obediently and hurried out.

Rodríguez pulled the information toward him, which included a photo of the blond woman who had been with Flores. He traced a finger over the lines of her beautiful face. "So, *Señorita* Freya Martinson, you enjoy Cuban men?" His smile widened. "Perhaps you and I can enjoy each other when I come to visit you."

18

MARCO THREW MORE OF Francisco's fancy modeling clothes into his bag. Good thing his brother was such a clotheshorse, since Marco hadn't exactly wanted to hang out at the Laundromat. Confessing his true background to Rey three days ago had drawn them even closer together. They had spent the entire time since Saturday holed up in her loft, finishing her sketches and making love.

Leaving her this morning, even for an hour as she fixed them breakfast, was terribly painful. How was he supposed to leave her tonight? But he'd pushed their luck far enough and his continued presence would only drag her further into danger.

Marco also grabbed the red-and-black cardboard box that held his spare ammunition. He wasn't sure if he'd be back to the apartment and he didn't want to leave anything incriminating behind. Next to the box was another untraceable cell phone.

Before he left Chicago, he needed to talk to Eddie. His friend had promised to poke around at the office and track down anything new.

His call went through immediately. "Jones here." From the engine noise, Eddie was driving his big diesel pickup on one of South Florida's freeways.

"Lalo, it's me."

"Goddamn, it's good to hear from you. The shit's hit the fan here." His friend's Texan accent thickened with emotion.

"What the hell happened?" Marco stopped messing with sweaters and concentrated on his friend's information.

"They found one of our computer geeks in the swamp with his throat cut. What little blood he had left was full of cocaine, and his bank statements had some mysterious deposits starting right before your cover got blown. They're going over his PC with a fine-tooth comb, but it'll take a while to break the encryption."

Marco swore a long, foul stream of Spanish obscenities. "Damn it all, that prick got my informant killed and nearly got me and my family, too."

"*Amigo,* I hope you're in a different city than the last time you called me." Eddie's voice was muffled as he shoved a cigarette into his mouth and clicked his lighter.

"I will be tomorrow." Marco wanted to curse his own break in professionalism, but a selfish part of him couldn't regret falling in love with Rey.

Eddie coughed. "Buddy, get your ass outta there! And try to change your look. You still have that mess of hair?"

"It's going right now."

"Good. Shit, I'm pulling into the office now. I was here until two last night and they called me in for a nine-o'clock meeting, probably about *you.*"

"I am sorry, Lalo, for getting you involved." He'd dragged yet another person into his mess. "I don't want you in trouble with the bosses, too."

"Aw, hell with them. Call me later today if you can. I'll try to get a fix on Rodríguez for you." Eddie hung up.

Marco ran his fingers through his hair and cursed as he found yet another tangle. He couldn't untangle all the snarls in his life, but by God, his hair was one thing he *could* fix. He gathered his supplies.

Five minutes later he laid paper towels in the sink and plugged in the clippers he'd found in a closet. He flicked on the switch, the raspy hum reverberating off the tiny bathroom's tile walls. He stared at his reflection and ran the clipper right down the middle of his head. No turning back with only an inch of hair left. He made quick work of the rest of his curls, shaving his head like a penitent about to ask forgiveness for his sins.

A familiar face stared at him. This was the Marco Flores he really knew. The Marco who had never helped ship drugs into his adopted country. The Marco who had never held a man down while thugs beat him. The Marco who had never witnessed the murder of a drug rival and had been powerless to stop it for risk of blowing his cover.

With most of his hair lying in the sink, his head felt lighter, but his heart grew heavy. He was about to leave the only woman he had ever loved without knowing when he would be back. But he knew one thing. If he had breath in his body, he would return to her.

REY LET OUT A CURSE AS her German-steel paring knife got stuck in a mango for the third time. What kind of huge pit did that fruit have anyway? The buzzer sounded, and she wiped her hands on a linen dish towel before pressing the button. "Yes?"

"Rey, it's me." It was Marco.

"I'll be right there." She jumped from the kitchen bar stool, eager to see him.

She yanked the door open and closed it behind him. "Are you all right?" She anxiously examined what she could see of him. Now she understood why he'd always covered his entire face outdoors, even on relatively mild days.

"I'm fine." He shed his scarf, coat and sunglasses, leaving his hat for last.

When he finally pulled it off, a sick pain shot through her stomach. "My God. What did you do?"

"My hair?" He gave her a sheepish look. A sheep shorn to within an inch of its life.

"Yes, your hair!" His beautiful black curls were gone. The inch-long stubble was slicked back with some gel, outlining the perfect oval shape of his skull.

"I needed a change." His voice was uncompromising. "I couldn't stand that long hair anymore."

Rey realized he wasn't a professional model, but she never thought he would cut his hair like a Marine going into boot camp. "I'm just glad I finished the sketches of your head."

He looked surprised. "I'm sorry, Reina. I never thought of that." He came closer. "Did I ruin it for you?"

"No," she admitted. "I have just a few sketches of your arms and legs left." She ran her hand over his scalp. "But oh, your beautiful hair."

"If you like my hair longer, I can grow it. But no more Shirley Temple ringlets." He grabbed her hand and kissed it. "Mmm. You smell sweet and juicy."

Rey's knees almost buckled as he sucked her index

finger into his mouth and circled his tongue around it. He steadied her and moved his tongue to her middle finger. He released her finger. "Delicious. Do you have any more juicy, succulent fruit for me to suck on?"

Her breasts grew heavy and warm, her nipples pressing painfully against her lacy bra. "I'm fixing some mangoes for after dinner, but they're ruining my good knife." She walked into the kitchen to get the fruit pulp off her hands before she smeared it all over him.

"Mangoes?" He pronounced it the Spanish way—*mahn-goes.* "I didn't know you liked mangoes."

"I've never had them before. Do you like mangoes?" She displayed the two unmangled mangoes for his inspection.

"Of course." He covered her hands with his. "Especially the plump ones that overflow your palms. The flesh is firm but resilient when you squeeze it."

Rey withdrew her hands and set the fruit on the counter. "You must be quite the connoisseur."

"Most Cuban men love mangoes—practically from birth. What else did you buy?"

"Some little red bananas and some larger bananas that had yellow peels but were too tough to eat."

He looked at the bowl of fruit. "Those are plantains. You need to fry them first to soften them."

"Oh."

He hastened to reassure her. "Don't worry. It was nice of you to buy this."

"I also bought a papaya."

"Papaya?" A naughty gleam sparked in his eyes. "Now that is my favorite."

She looked at him. He must be more homesick than she thought. Or maybe he was vitamin C deficient.

"Here, let me finish slicing those for you," he offered, hefting the knife. "Good balance." He tossed the knife end-over-end above his head, blade flashing.

Rey shrieked.

He caught the knife handle neatly and peeled a mango. "What?"

"What are you trying to do, cut off your fingers?" Her heart was pounding out of her chest. She'd never seen him be so reckless before, as if he didn't care what happened to him.

"Now why would I do that? My fingers have very important work to do first." He leaned over to kiss her, but she pulled away, self-conscious of the splotches of fruit pulp covering her rumpled white shirt.

"Don't go, Reina. I promise not to throw knives anymore."

"No, I'll let you finish slicing the fruit while I change. Besides, where did you learn to throw knives? Secret-agent school?" She tried to make a joke.

"Defending myself from Miami cockroaches. Those *cucarachas* grow as big as grapefruits."

Rey shuddered. "No, seriously."

His expression darkened briefly and then he smiled at her with some effort. "I am serious." He cut the mango into cubes and separated them off the big flat seed. "Miami can be a very dangerous city."

After his revelations the past few days she understood that very well.

He speared a cube of mango with the knife tip and ate it off the blade, scooping the fruit into a cobalt-blue stoneware bowl. "Now go change your clothes before I strip them off you right here in the kitchen." He rinsed the much-vaunted papaya with her brushed-nickel sink sprayer.

Rey slipped into her bedroom and stared unseeing into her closet. His haircut had emphasized a different side of his personality, one that she had glimpsed when he'd manhandled Stefan and when he'd rushed her into hiding at the salsa club.

Pulling off her top and jeans, she frowned. The fruit juice had soaked through her white cotton shirt, sticking her bra to her breasts. She unhooked the clasp and peeled the white satin from her skin, rummaging through her low-slung pale maple dresser for a clean bra. She picked up a black lace demicup bra and admired the effect in the mirror above her dresser. Looking good in dark colors was probably the only advantage of having skin the color of a Norwegian cod's belly.

"Knock, knock." Rey's gaze flew to the mirror. Marco stood behind her in the open doorway.

"I didn't hear you." She felt strangely vulnerable, exposed back and front by the mirror. Her nipples hardened under his intense gaze and scraped against the black lace.

He set a tray on her nightstand and came up behind her. "You don't need this." He plucked the bra out of her hands and tossed it aside.

Her breasts hung free for a brief moment until he covered them with his hands. His fingers plucked at her nipples, twanging sensations to her wet center.

She leaned on his hard chest, letting his hands mold and cup her breasts, her greedy flesh overflowing his palms. His wet mouth nipped hungrily at her neck, and she wiggled her bottom against his swelling cock.

"Open your eyes," he commanded. She dragged her lids open, staring hazily at their entwined reflection. "You remind me of a beach in the Florida Keys, deserted except for the birds and dolphins. See how blue your eyes become when I touch you, like the sky above. Your hair is soft and golden like the sand. And here—" he ran a finger across the silk of her panties "—is the sea, warm, wet and salty."

She widened her stance, allowing him access to her throbbing center. He released her breasts and scooped her into his arms, setting her on the soft goose-down duvet.

The plump coverlet cradled her body. She reached for Marco to pull him down next to her, but he sat at the edge of the bed. "Are you hungry?" he asked.

"Not for food."

"Oh, you'll be full when I finish."

She shivered, imagining how he could fill her.

"Lie down, Rey." He kicked off his Italian-leather loafers and turned to sit cross-legged on the bed. He ignored the erection tenting the zipper of his khakis and reached for a cloth-covered plate. "I brought you some mango."

She propped herself on her elbows and he slipped a pale orange cube of fruit into her mouth. "Mmm, that's good." It tasted exotic and fresh.

He selected another piece of mango and brushed it over her lips. She licked a drop of nectar, but he didn't let her eat the mango. Instead he rubbed it over her chin and traced it along the column of her neck. His hot tongue lapped the juice that pooled at the hollow of her throat.

"Did I ever tell you why Cuban men love mangoes?" He had a devilish look on his face.

"Don't Cuban women?"

He smiled slyly. "*Mangoes* are Cuban slang for breasts." Rey's gasp of outrage turned into a gasp of a different kind as he slid another cube of mango over her breast and swirled it around her turgid nipple.

"You men. Are breasts all you think about?" It was difficult to manufacture indignation when the slick fruit was sending jolts of pleasure from her nipples to her pulsing cleft.

"Why not? You don't seem to mind my attentions." A sweet, exotic scent filled her bedroom as he crushed the mango in his palm. Juice oozed between his fingers and she watched the peach-colored rivulets run over her throbbing pink nipples and the pale skin of her breasts. He opened his hand and spread the pulp over her left breast. Rey arched as his wet, sticky hand slipped over her hot skin. He bent his head and nipped her breast with his teeth, making her squeal. He lifted his head and licked his lips.

"Mangoes are ripe and juicy like your breasts. Tender flesh that I can nibble on." He squeezed another fistful of mango cubes and smeared them over her other breast. He rubbed his open mouth over her skin, sipping the fruit juice. He cupped one of her breasts in his hand and fastened his mouth over one of her pulp-strewn nipples. Rey moaned as his clever tongue swirled around her areola, licking her clean. He spread more crushed pulp on the aching tip and nibbled at her with his teeth. She squirmed frantically, trying to get him to touch the needy ache between her thighs, but he ignored her pleas and moved his teasing mouth to her other nipple, sucking and lapping at her swollen flesh.

He sat on his heels and she gasped in protest as his mouth left her breasts. Heedless of his sticky hands, he yanked the silk crewneck sweater over his head, exposing his tight pecs and lean abs. Although she'd photographed and sketched every inch of him, she still grew weak at the sight of his chest, lightly sprinkled with black hair. His erection was even larger, bulging against the front of his pants. She tried to reach for his belt buckle, heedless of anything but freeing his cock to plunge deep inside her aching center.

"I told you to lie down." His tone was stern, but his touch was gentle as he pushed her onto the pillows. He grabbed two big linen napkins off the tray, and she thought he would wipe the mango off her breasts. Instead he rolled them into long cylinders and looped them around her wrists.

Was he doing what she thought he was doing? "Marco, I don't have any fruit on my arms."

He tugged one wrist up and tied it to the headboard. "Marco!" She tugged at the knot, trying to ignore the fresh flush of desire as he tied up her other wrist. She lay flat, her vulnerable breasts tipped up and swinging free. "Don't you want me to touch you?"

"No. I haven't finished eating your mangoes." He lowered himself on top of her and rubbed his chest against her breasts, up and down, side to side. Her sticky nipples caught and rasped against the crisp black hair sprinkling his pecs.

He nuzzled the undersides of her breasts and dipped his tongue in the hollow under her sternum. He traced a line down to her belly button and dipped his tongue in. "Yum. Sweet." She scooted her body higher on her bed, trying to get his mouth on top of her throbbing core. Her tiny thong panties were unbearably tight, her swollen lower folds and clitoris pressing against the black lace. He rubbed his long finger against her seam, circling briefly around the knot of nerves at the top.

He raised his head and grinned. "I'm still hungry." He stood up off the bed.

Rey cursed a particularly vile Swedish epithet and kicked at him.

"I don't understand what you said, but I got the gist of it." He pulled two more napkins off the tray. Rey watched him warily. Her breasts were still sticky, and she thought he had other plans rather than wiping her off.

He grabbed one ankle and tied it to the foot of her bed. Rey twisted and tried to kick at him with her other foot, but she got no leverage and he ducked her easily, fastening her other ankle to the other bedpost. "And this is the thanks I get for slaving away in a hot kitchen to fix you a snack."

"You're the only one eating anything."

He leered at her. "And aren't you lucky?"

Rey squirmed but she couldn't get free. "Untie me, Marco. I've never done this before." She'd had a few weird bondage offers from people on the fringe element of the art scene but had always refused them.

His fruit-sweetened breath scorched her cheek. "I think you like being tied up, Reina."

A hot flush rose from her bare, sticky breasts all the way to her tousled hair, and she looked away from his knowing glance.

"You always have the position of power with men, not only in your artwork but because you're so beautiful."

"I don't think I'm that beautiful."

"Rey, *querida,* you almost made me come when I first auditioned for you. Always looking, never touching. God, you must have had nerves of steel."

"No, I could hardly keep myself from kneeling down and licking you," she admitted, the memory bringing a rush through her overheated body.

He closed his eyes and gritted his teeth. "You're trying to drive me crazy, but I won't let you. Not yet. Now it's time for me to drive you crazy."

It *was* really sexy being spread wide open, the cool air swirling around her exposed thighs and teasing her hot cleft. She wiggled her hips, the thong riding deep into her dripping folds. It didn't help. She needed him to touch her.

He stretched out one muscular arm to grab another plate of sliced fruit.

"Is that more mango?" Rey tugged on her linen bonds, but she was trussed like a Swedish Christmas goose. She stifled a laugh. Mother had insisted on giving her the table linens, saying Rey's reliance on paper napkins was tacky. At least Marco couldn't have tied her up with paper napkins.

"No. This is papaya. Another Cuban favorite." He held a slice of papaya to her lips and she took a bite. The soft fruit smashed on her tongue, bathing it with exotic juices.

"That's delicious. Now untie me and take off your pants."

He stood and loosened his slim black leather belt.

As he undid his zipper, the hot bulge of his erection pushed against the straining waistband of his briefs. "I'll untie you but not yet. I haven't even made you come screaming my name." Rey's stomach jumped half from nerves and half from excitement. What would it be like to be totally vulnerable to this darker, more dangerous Marco, to let him do whatever he wanted to her while she couldn't touch him?

He took her silence for acquiescence and ate a slice of papaya. "Delicious." He licked each one of his long fingers, sucking the juice off every fingertip. "Have you ever seen what a papaya looks like on the inside, Reina?"

"No, I've never opened one."

"Most women haven't. You're lucky I'm here to take care of your papaya, Rey. Cuban men are the best in the world." He picked up a papaya half, pear-shaped but a tiny bit bigger. The narrow neck of its glistening rosy-orange flesh was divided in two by its core, opening into an oval hollow below.

Rey stared at his wicked grin. "Oh, my God. *Papaya* is some sort of slang for…for…" Her voice trailed off as she searched for words.

"Want some?" he offered. "It's really juicy and sweet." He held the papaya to his face and licked the center of the fruit, his eyes never leaving hers.

She felt that lick as if his tongue had been on her instead of the fruit. Moisture trickled between her thighs like the papaya juice dripping down Marco's chin. She squirmed to ease the pressure between her legs, but her ankles were spread too far apart. She still wasn't sure about been tied up, so she took refuge in sarcasm. "What is it with Cuban men and fruit? Do you get a boner shopping in the produce department?"

"No fruit is as sweet as you, Reina. I'd rather eat your papaya."

He laid the half papaya on the plate and chose a slice. "But I think the combination would be very tasty." He knelt between her widespread legs and pulled aside her thong, murmuring in Spanish.

"What did you say?" It was hard for her to breathe, watching him gaze at her innermost secrets.

"You have a beautiful papaya, *mi amor.*"

She gasped as he traced her folds with the slice of fruit, painting her liberally with its juice. All of the blood in her body had flowed to her center, swelling and throbbing there while she got dizzy and light-headed. Up and down, back and forth, he slid the papaya around her sex, coming close to her aching bud but never touching it. Rey tossed her head on her luxurious nest of pillows, the heat and pressure building. He finally rubbed the fruit on her clitoris, causing her hips to thrust wildly against his hand.

He groaned and tossed the fruit away. Rey heard it splat against the hardwood floor but didn't care.

"Let me taste your sweetness, *querida.*" With a sharp tug he snapped the black lace pressing against her clit and shoved the fabric away. He dipped his newly shorn black head, the short hair rasping against the tender skin of her thighs. The heat of his tongue scorched the pulsing knot of nerves and she screamed his name.

He slipped a finger inside her, probing and stretching her. He slipped in a second finger, and her tiny muscles clenched and quivered. He raised his head to stare at her. He reminded her of a photo she'd seen of a black jaguar interrupted mid-drink at the Amazon River, amber eyes glittering, mouth glistening. Trapped in his savage gaze, she shivered.

Then he smiled and the savageness melted away. "You like that, don't you?" His fingers slid even deeper, pressing against a particularly sensitive spot. She ground her hips against him. "Marco, please! I want you inside me."

"Not yet." He bent his head and swirled his tongue around and around her aching bud. Her legs quivered from straining against the fine linen bonds. His mouth lapped at her, hot and wet, coaxing every drop of response from her that she had to give. Just as she couldn't bear the buildup of sensation, he darted his tongue inside her, giving her tiny muscles something to clench on. The dam broke and an exquisite flood washed over her, leaving her limp and drained.

She heaved a sigh of contentment and raised an eyebrow. "I enjoyed the lesson on naughty Cuban slang, but it seems one-sided. There has to be a nickname for the penis."

He gave her a wicked smile. "Of course there is. I saved that lesson for last. *Pepino* is a nickname for the penis, but it really means 'cucumber.'"

"That makes sense."

"I know you love to eat cucumbers." He stood and slowly pushed down his briefs. His erection sprang free, almost touching his tight abs. Desire coiled between her thighs again. He was so sexy it almost hurt to look at him. What would she do when he was gone? She decided to play it cool. "You do, hmm? How do you know that?" She wiggled into her nest of pillows.

"You love to eat my *pepino*." He straddled her belly, rubbing his penis between her breasts. If she tipped her head, she could suck him deep into her mouth just as in the sauna.

"Marco!" She blushed but couldn't deny it. His erection had made her mouth water from the first time she'd seen him strip off his briefs and pose for her.

"And I found something in your refrigerator that gave me an idea." To her utter disappointment he swung off her.

"What? Whipped cream? Jelly? Honey?" Maybe he'd play with her breasts some more.

He lifted a cloth napkin. "A *pepino*." A whole hothouse cucumber lay on the tray, long and thick. Its smooth, waxy, green skin glistened in the candlelight.

"Marco, I'm really not hungry anymore. And it's not even peeled and sliced."

"But I did wash it." He admired the vegetable, turning it around in his hand. "Sad to say, my *pepino* is not this big."

"You'd have trouble walking. That thing is almost a foot long."

"It's easy to see the comparison. Long and thick but smooth with a rounded tip, meant for gliding in and out of a woman's body." He hefted the cucumber.

"Marco, are you talking about you or the cucumber?" She shivered as he traced the outline of her nipples with the icy vegetable. He dragged it down the center of her belly until it rested right above her mound.

"Both." He grinned up at her.

"Both?" she squeaked. He couldn't mean what she thought he meant.

"Sí." He parted her lower lips with his thumb and forefinger. *"Dios mío,"* he said in mock concern. "Your papaya is all pink and swollen. Was I too rough?"

She grew even more swollen as he petted her moist flesh. "No," she whimpered.

"Are you sure? I can see you getting even pinker just lying here. Let me check." He slipped one finger inside her and she spasmed around him. He withdrew his finger and spread her juices over her clitoris. "I couldn't tell with just one finger. I'd better try again." He wiggled two fingers inside her, stretching her.

Her hands clutched at empty air, straining against their bonds. "Stop teasing me."

"Do you ache?"

She nodded, aching badly for him.

"I think you need something cool and soothing." He pulled his fingers out of her and rubbed the cucumber against her throbbing cleft.

"Marco!" Her eyes flew open. "That's cold."

He stopped immediately and she moaned. "Touch me more."

Leaning over to nibble her neck, he whispered, "First, this *pepino*. If you're still hungry afterward, I'll let you eat *my pepino*."

"Don't you want to push your cock inside me and come?" She had a brief victory when his erection jerked and left a damp trail against her thigh, but he shook his head.

"You want to try this, I can tell. It's long and thick and smooth," he cajoled, twisting the cucumber against the rim of her passage.

"I don't know about this."

He pulled it back abruptly. "This is the only *pepino* you're going to get."

She sucked in a deep breath and glared at him. She couldn't even kick him out of her bed and finish by herself.

"Tell me what you want." He was relentless, nudging her clitoris with tiny rhythmic strokes. Her feverish body heat was starting to warm the cucumber's tip.

"Yes," she muttered.

"What?" he asked, slipping in the cucumber an inch or so. She gasped as her tiny muscles clenched around it. He pulled it out, waiting for her answer.

She gritted her teeth. "Yes, all right, damn it. Give me the *pepino.*"

He thrust it inside her. Cold filling her heat. Totally stretching her swollen tissues. She arched her back off the bed and screamed in pleasure. "Oh, my God, Marco!"

He slowly pulled it out again, making her whimper in frustration, then wiggled it into her, inch by agonizing inch.

He slowly rotated the cucumber deep inside her, filling her harder and thicker than she'd ever had before. She writhed against her linen bonds, the silky duvet slipping against her back and bottom.

"Are you close?"

She nodded, her breath searing her throat in large gasps as she shut her eyes.

"Good. Let's take you all the way there." He bent his head and sucked her clitoris hard into his mouth. The hot, wet suction of his mouth and the cold, hard pressure of the cucumber against her vagina sparked bursts of colors. Mango-orange, papaya-pink and cucumber-green swirled on the black canvas of her closed eyelids, pulling her into a world of uncontrolled chromatic overload where she was the painting and Marco was the artist.

As she blinked to clear her vision, he lifted his gleaming mouth. She moaned in frustration as he eased the cucumber out of her still-pulsing sheath.

"Don't worry, *querida*. We're not done yet."

She sighed with relief as he pushed inside her. After the vegetable's chill, his bare cock was blazing hot.

She saw him grit his teeth as she contracted around him. He muttered in Spanish as he thrust in and out of her, his chest rubbing her fruit-sticky breasts. Already sensitized from her first two orgasms, her innermost muscles tightened as the pressure from his penis rubbed against her clitoris and his balls slapped her wet flesh. She squirmed against her bonds, wanting more, wanting to touch him as he came.

He paused for a second and freed her wrists and ankles. Rey immediately threw her legs onto his shoulders, gasping as his cock penetrated even deeper into her throbbing flesh.

"*Tócate, tócate,*" he said with a groan. "Touch yourself, *mi amor.*" His hair-roughened chest abraded the backs of her thighs as he increased his tempo.

She slipped her hand between their sweat-slicked bodies, her fingertips stroking him as he pushed in and out of her. Her index finger found the swollen nub between them and circled it, first slowly, than quickly as the tension built. "Oh, Marco," she crooned, cupping her breast in her other hand. "Taste me."

He bent his head and nipped the tip of her breast. The

silken thread of desire connecting her nipple and her vagina snapped, and she came again, arching as she feverishly caressed herself.

He threw back his head with a loud groan, the tendons in his neck standing out like steel cords. He thrust deep into her wet depths. "Oh, Reina, I love you, I love you."

"I love you, too." She held him close as he slumped onto her, his heavy body pinning her to the fruit-stained coverlet.

They lay together in the cozy nest of her bed for several minutes. Rey stroked his head, the short black hairs tickling her fingers.

He finally raised his head and smiled at her. "Sweetheart." He tried to roll off her and they both yelped.

"I think I lost a few chest hairs." He examined her breasts. The streaks of mango pulp had hardened to the consistency of rubber cement.

She sat up and rubbed her own chest as he flopped onto the bed. "It feels like I peeled my breasts off a Naughahyde couch in summertime."

"Have you ever done that?"

"Done what?" She glanced over her shoulder at him.

He leered at her. "Had to peel your lush, naked tits off sweaty vinyl furniture?"

She laughed. "No, Marco, I've never had to do that."

"Too bad. My mother has this poolside lounge chair that would be perfect. You put on a sexy black bikini and lie down while I rub lotion all over you." He moved behind her and caressed her back with long, sweeping strokes.

"Ooh, I get it. I've always wanted to play Rich Tourist and Cabana Boy."

He purposely deepened his Cuban accent. "You don't

want to get tan lines, *señorita*. Shall I gallantly untie your bikini top?"

"Marco, I've never tanned dark enough to even get a tan line. And where's my piña colada?"

"Shh." He pinched her bottom and she yelped. "This is my fantasy. So I untie your bikini bottom and begin smoothing lotion over your fantastic ass." He pushed her gently to her stomach, caressing her bottom. She wiggled a little, opening her legs wider.

"As you lie naked and glistening on the lounge chair, I cannot contain my desire any longer."

She tipped her head back in pleasure, but her long hair snarled on the drying fruit juices on his hands. "Ouch! Time to go wash off this fruit salad."

He heaved a disgruntled sigh. "Poor cabana boy. I bet she forgets to tip him, too."

She cupped her breasts, pressing them together. "When I come back, you can show me how a horny blond foreigner might please a Cuban cabana boy." She licked her lips slowly, enjoying how his pupils dilated sharply, only a narrow rim of gold surrounding the black. "Is Cuban-style on the drink menu?"

He growled deep in his throat and reached for her, but she scrambled off the bed, laughing. "I have to get this fruit off my skin before it dries permanently."

"You just wait, Reina. We'll go lie by my mother's pool in Miami and I'll make you come screaming on that lounge chair."

She trotted into the bathroom. "Only if you serve me a piña colada."

"I'll *serve* you plenty," he called after her.

She stood under the hot spray of water and scrubbed

at the mango with her shower puff and creamy jasmine body wash. Turning off the water, she slipped into her pink robe and heard him rattling around in the kitchen. "Still hungry?" she teased.

"Just being a good cabana boy and clearing away the dishes." He came around the corner wearing the dark blue robe. She'd have to buy a new robe for her next model since she'd never be able to let anyone else wear it. "There's fruit on the sheets though."

"I'll change them while you wash off." She pushed him toward the shower. "Later we can play Cabana Boy in the sauna. No vinyl furniture but plenty of heat."

"Excellent." He stepped into the bathroom, where she heard him humming a tune from the salsa club.

She went to her small linen closet for a new set of sheets and found Marco's open bag sitting in front of it, stuffed to the gills with clothes. Everything was neatly rolled and folded, as if he had packed for a long trip instead of an overnight stay at her loft.

His dark, reckless mood made sense now. He was planning to leave her, probably first thing tomorrow or even as soon as it got dark.

Well, she wasn't going to lie weeping alone on her chaise, wondering if he was alive or dead. Whatever happened, she would be with him. She grabbed her own suitcase from under her bed and tossed in underwear and long johns.

She heard Marco come out of the bathroom behind her. "Reina, what are you doing?"

She fisted her hands on her hips and turned to glare at him. "Packing to come with you. Do I need winter clothes or summer clothes?"

19

MARCO'S FRESHLY SHAVED jaw dropped. "Come with me? *Ay, Dios mío,* are you *loca?* You can't come with me!"

"If that means am I crazy, then no, I'm not crazy. But I am coming with you, wherever you go." Rey pulled some turtlenecks from her drawer and shoved them into her bag.

"No! I absolutely forbid it." His accent had thickened with emotion and he yanked her bag away from her.

"Forbid it?" She pointed at the table linens still dangling from her bedposts. "You'll have to tie me up with those napkins again to keep me here."

Marco tossed her bag into a corner. "Don't tempt me! It's too dangerous to be with me anymore. Rodríguez would take pleasure in your suffering because it would make me suffer, as well."

She crossed her arms over her breasts. "You know I'm not safe here, either. What am I supposed to do if he tracks you here and finds me alone? Stab him with my chisel?"

"I don't know!" He paced across the floor, the robe flapping around his legs. "Go to Meg's apartment. Go travel with your parents overseas. Just let me go alone."

"No." She caught him midstep, wrapping her arms

around his chest. "Did you mean what you said about spending the rest of your life with me?"

He sighed, pulling her close and nuzzling her damp hair. "It may not be a very long life, *querida*."

"Whatever happens, we'll be together." She settled into his embrace with relief.

"I'll do my best to protect both of us." He clasped her shoulders and stared at her, his hazel eyes fierce. "But you must do everything I tell you."

She nodded eagerly. "I will."

"I mean it." He shook her gently. "If I tell you to run away and leave me, you have to obey me. I lived with these savages for over a year. I know what they are capable of."

"I could never leave you, Marco...."

He interrupted her with an angry shout. "Promise me or I *will* tie you up and leave you here!"

She shivered. Her previous romantic notions of dark, dangerous men were very silly now that they were faced with real danger. "Where will we go?"

He thought hard. "We'll go south through Indiana and swing up into Michigan. There are dozens of small towns and back roads there."

"And if we carry my old skis and ice skates, we'll look like winter tourists."

"Good idea." He quickly dressed. "I need to get that car. You have an hour to get ready."

"Be careful." She clung to him, his muscles rock-hard from tension.

"I will. Pack warm, but pack light. And make sure your loft is shut down tight. We may not be back for a long while." He bundled himself up and stepped into the dazzling sunshine.

She locked the door behind him and ran into her bedroom, retrieving her bag. She dressed and braided her hair, then quickly packed a couple pairs of jeans, long underwear, some turtlenecks and her heaviest wool sweater. She found an extra-large sweater and tossed it in for Marco. Those stylish cashmere knits he wore would be no match for the cold north woods.

She tossed the bag near the door. Forty-five minutes left. She stuffed her sketches of Marco into a mailing tube and addressed them to her agent. At this point she didn't care when or even if Evelyn got them. Nothing else mattered but keeping Marco safe.

Rey looked around the loft to make sure all her appliances and heaters were turned off. A wistful smile crossed her face as she saw the oil painting of Marco sitting on her easel.

She'd painted him nude, lying on the chaise longue where they'd first made love. The hard lines of his bronze body gleamed from the soft swath of white cloth. But her painting wasn't quite finished, her expensive brushes crusting over with drying oil paints. She checked the clock. Half an hour. It would only take five minutes to clean her brushes. Painting in oils gave wonderfully luminous color, but the cleanup was messy and required turpentine or other smelly solvents.

She opened the metal can of paint thinner. There was only a dab at the bottom, not enough to clean her brushes, since it had been several months since she last painted in oil. Setting that can aside, she unscrewed the cap of the turpentine container. The fumes blasted out, burning the inside of her nose. Oh, well. It was either turpentine or risk ruining hundreds of dollars worth of brushes. And when she came back she probably wouldn't have any money to replace them.

The buzzer sounded. She wasn't expecting anyone but Marco, but just to be on the safe side, she pressed the intercom button. "Marco?"

"Sí, querida." His voice was muffled from that scarf he always wore outdoors.

She smiled. She'd learned from Marco that *querida* meant *darling.* He used it often. She dashed over to the door and yanked it open.

"Señorita Freya Martinson." An older man stood on the stoop, swaddled in an exorbitantly expensive cashmere coat. He had a thick fur hat pulled low on his brow, and his jaw and neck were wrapped in a fine wool scarf.

She tried to slam the door closed, but he shouldered his way inside the loft.

"Get out!" She ran for her phone to call 911. He easily cut off her escape route, shoving her toward her easel.

"I see I have found the right place." He pulled off his hat and scarf, revealing a neatly trimmed head of salt-and-pepper hair. His face was lined but still handsome in a craggy way. He surveyed the contents of her loft, stopping when he saw the painting of Marco. "Your current project?"

"If you leave now, I won't call the cops. I don't have any money or drugs here." She tried to bluff him.

"Señorita, I have all the drugs and money I could ever want." He turned his stare on her full-force for the first time and she took an involuntary step back. His eyes were pale, pale green, almost yellow. "I'd prefer to stay and look at your artwork. And perhaps meet your model." His raspy voice had the same accent as Marco.

She shook her head, frantically thinking. "I used a reference photo to paint from. No model."

"I will wait for him." He advanced toward her. Rey retreated. "I think Marco Santiago Flores will come back to you, given the proper incentive."

A chill ran down her spine. He knew Marco's full name. She was the only person in Chicago who knew his full name. She bumped against the countertop where she had been cleaning her brushes and reached behind her for the razor knife she used to cut her canvases.

Gripping the knife handle, she waved it at him. "No one comes to my home and threatens me."

He laughed. "Such a *tigresa*. No wonder Flores has been sniffing around you."

He pounced on her with the swiftness of a wild animal. Metal clanged and glass shattered on her workbench. She didn't have time to scream before he was grinding her wrist in his painful clasp. Her heart pounded frantically as he forced her grip open.

The knife clattered to the floor. She swung her left fist at his head, clipping him on the jaw. He slipped in a puddle and went down on one knee.

She tugged futilely at his strong grasp. He was so close she could see the cold glitter in his eyes.

"Muy bien." He shook off her punch and stood. "Did Flores tell you I like women who fight me? Just ask his *mamá*."

So this was the man who'd tried to rape Marco's mother. She glared at him. "A real man doesn't need to force a woman."

His return stare was yellow and feral. He increased the pressure, bending her hand at an obscene angle.

"How many statues will you sculpt after hand surgery?" She moaned as he twisted her wrist another few degrees. "I've found that torn tendons and ligaments heal much more slowly than broken bones."

She panicked and kicked at his crotch. He twisted away.

"Ah, ah, ah," he chided. His pinky ring split her lip and she tasted coppery blood.

He forced her to her knees and smiled at her. "I can see why Flores stayed here instead of moving on. You are quite appealing in that position."

"You can scuttle under whatever rock you came from." She forced the brave words through the lump in her throat.

"What a mouth you have." He looked amused. "If only I had more time, I would put it to better use."

Rey tried a rational tone of voice, although she knew she was dealing with an irrational man. "If you leave now, I won't call the cops."

He actually laughed. "I have Colombian cartels to answer to. Do you think your Chicago Police Department worries me?"

The loft door rattled open. "Reina, we have to get out of here! Eddie said Rodríguez is on his way—" He froze in horror for a split second.

"Marco, watch out!"

He was already drawing his steel-gray pistol and spinning into a crouch.

Rodríguez released her wrists and wrenched her to her feet. Yanking on her braid, he slammed her against him.

"So, Flores, back to where we started." The drug lord's breath was hot and stale. She struggled, but he held fast.

"With you hiding behind a woman?" Marco's tone was cool, the pistol never wavering. Rodríguez's arm tightened across her throat.

"Ah, yes. Your beautiful *mamá*. Such a ripe body. And those sweet lips of hers." He sighed in mock nostalgia and added a couple sentences in Spanish. She didn't understand the words, but the vulgar tone was clear.

Marco's knuckles whitened around the pistol grip. "I should have cut your throat on that raft when you were unconscious. *Mamá* said no."

"A woman of mercy."

Marco laughed coldly. "No. She almost did it herself until she realized a shark feeding frenzy might swamp the raft."

He stiffened with rage. "Enough!" he barked. "Toss that pistol over in the corner."

Marco's hand never wavered.

"Do it!" Rodríguez wrapped her braid around his fist and yanked her head sideways. Her neck muscles screamed from the awkward angle.

"Don't do it, Marco!" She couldn't see his face anymore, just the paint-stained concrete floor. "He wants to kill you!"

"You know me, Flores. I can snap her neck in one second."

"You'd be dead the next second."

"Are you going to risk your pretty blond whore? If you drop the gun, I might let her live. Not you, of course. You know too much."

Only the rasping of her breath broke the silence. Until she heard metal clatter against the floor. "No, Marco!" Hot tears blurred her eyes.

"What now, *Lobo?*"

Rey tensed her muscles to run to Marco.

"Please, *señorita,* stay here with me." A circle of metal pressed into her neck. She froze, the gun's chill pouring through her body.

"If you hurt her, I'll cut you up and feed you to the sharks. They don't have any qualms about eating their own." Marco's voice was cold and deadly, but she saw his face turn pale, his lips thinning.

"How touching." The older man laughed. "Your obvious affection for each other will only make my task more appealing." He released her hair and reached into his overcoat pocket. She panicked. Was it a knife this time? Instead he pulled out a roll of silver duct tape. "Look familiar, Flores? I brought the duct tape especially for you." He nudged Rey with the gun. "Walk slowly over to your lover and tape his wrists and ankles."

"What's the matter, Rodríguez? Are you afraid to come over here and do it yourself?" Marco's eyes glittered as he taunted the drug lord. "I taped you up myself on the raft and I was only twelve."

"Shut up!" Rey watched apprehensively as a purple vein bulged on his temple. "Now walk slowly and tape his wrists behind him."

Her shoes scuffed against the concrete as she crossed to Marco. Her eyes burned with unshed tears.

"It'll be all right, *corazón.*" He turned his back to her and brought his wrists together behind him. She started to tape around the thick cuffs of his coat, not touching his skin at all. Maybe he could slip his arms free.

"*Señorita* Freya, that is not exactly what I had in

mind." Rodríguez's sardonic voice stopped her covert maneuvers. "Pull off his coat and try again."

She bit her lip and pulled off his coat, wanting desperately to wrap her arms around him and hide them both.

"Do it, Reina." Marco's voice was cold and expressionless.

She found the end of the duct tape and wrapped his wrists together.

"Now lie on your stomach, Flores."

She threw the drug lord a hate-filled glance as Marco obeyed, dropping to his knees. She helped him ease down, his entire body rigid.

Rodríguez watched them with a glittering stare. She realized he was becoming sexually aroused. He slipped a hand into his trouser pocket and began stroking himself, and she almost gagged. Frantic, she looked for a weapon, a cell phone, anything, but he pointed the gun at Marco's head. "Tape his ankles to his wrists."

She froze. If Marco were bound hand and foot, he would be helpless. So would she.

Rodríguez cocked the gun. The hammer's harsh metallic click shattered the silence.

No. She would not be helpless. As long as she kept cool, she would save them. She bent to tape Marco's ankles, whispering encouragement to him.

"Perfect." The older man uncocked the pistol. "Come here."

She forced her wobbly legs to abandon Marco and return to their enemy, the stink of turpentine assaulting her nose as she drew near. The metal container had spilled onto the floor during their struggle. She realized with a savage glee that he'd stumbled into the combustible solvent when she'd knocked him over. Wet patches ruined his expensive pants and loafers.

Her small victory vanished as he put the gun down and stroked her cheek, his damp fingertips leaving trails of slime on her skin. "Give me the duct tape." His voice was low and intimate, a grotesque loverlike parody.

With Marco tied up on his stomach, their enemy obviously felt safe to assault her. She shook her head, recoiling. Could she reach the weapon before he did?

He read the direction of her stare. "Now, *querida,* if you took my pistol, would you even know how to use it?" He strapped her wrists together with several turns of duct tape.

The Spanish endearment sounded creepy coming from the older man instead of Marco. For the first time in her pacifistic Swedish life she wished she'd had formal weapons training. She wanted to kill him with her bare hands. "You're nothing but a low-life criminal." Maybe if she enraged him, he'd get careless.

"Shut your mouth before I shut it for you." He pulled off a six-inch length of tape and held it in front of her. "Before you condemn me, look at your boyfriend. He knew about at least three murders and even went along as backup for one."

Marco interrupted, "Reina, I was deep undercover. I pretended to go along until I had enough evidence for an indictment. The killings happened in the Caribbean, where I had no way to stop them."

"Who died?" Rey hoped to God it wasn't an innocent police officer or soldier.

The older man shrugged. "Rival dealers. Scum. The last one forced underage girls to smuggle in drugs and then sold them into prostitution. When my man Sánchez shot him, he was raping one of the girls."

He turned to Marco. "Thanks to me, Flores, you understand street justice. It's a good thing you won't live long enough to go back to your straight-arrow job with the *federales*."

"I'll live long enough to see you behind bars."

Rodríguez strode over to Marco and kicked him in the ribs. Marco flinched but didn't groan. "No more tracking down and killing street trash."

The drug lord grabbed Marco's forehead, forcing his head up into a contorted position. "You have the succulent taste of blood on your tongue. You have the sweet stench of fear in your nostrils as someone begs you for his life." His voice became a sibilant hiss. Marco's face turned purple from the increasing pressure on his neck. "You can never go back. You have become what you hate."

"That's not true! He's not like you!"

Rey shrank away as he dropped Marco's head and walked toward her with the strip of duct tape.

"Not yet anyway. After all, Flores stopped Sánchez from shooting the girl. Said he wanted a piece of her first. I suppose you smuggled her to safety, didn't you?"

"Far from the likes of you." Marco's voice was husky, but his color had subsided to his normal tan.

"Now, now, you of all people know I like my women nice and round and mature. Like your *mamá*. Like your girlfriend." He turned to her and wadded up the strip of tape, his eyes glowing. "On second thought, I won't tape your mouth. I can think of several *other* things to do with it." He shoved her and she stumbled onto the chaise, perching on the edge.

"Keep your damn hands off her!" Marco rolled on-to his side with a thud, muscles bulging futilely against his bonds.

Rey shuddered, thinking frantically. He'd given her an idea with his nasty innuendo. "How about a drink?" she asked brightly. Her mother had left a bot-tle of sleeping pills the last time she visited. Rey had just tossed them into one of her kitchen cabinets. Could she slip some into his drink? "I have whiskey, vodka and that Cuban beer with the Indian on the la-bel." Her voice trailed off as she remembered how she and Marco had shared a bottle of Hatuey beer right before they made love for the first time. They would share another bottle as soon as she beat that murder-ous bastard.

Her thoughts must have shown on her face because he laughed. "Forgive me my suspicious nature, but I must decline your hospitality. However, there is some-thing I've been wanting to do." He turned his attention to the vest pocket of his overcoat. She was dumbfound-ed at what he removed.

A long, fat cigar that looked like a stick of dynamite and would be just as deadly.

Marco groaned. "Those damn cigars of yours." His voice was tight and worried.

"Damn cigars?" Rodríguez smirked. "I'll have you know these are hand-rolled to my personal specifica-tions by the fine workers of Cuba." He trimmed the end of the cigar with tiny gold scissors and produced a heavy gold lighter from the same pocket.

"No, stop! You can't smoke in here!" The odor of tur-pentine was strong enough to choke on. What was the matter with the man? Couldn't he smell the fumes? She looked at Marco. He shook his head.

"Ah, you Americans and your antismoking." Rodríguez chuckled indulgently. "Afraid I'm going to pollute the air of your precious loft?"

"You polluted it by just coming here." Rey couldn't let him light that cigar.

His face hardened. "Or maybe you just want to get down to business. Find out what you've been missing."

"Just let him smoke the damn thing, Rey. Mouth cancer is a painful death." Marco flicked his glance between her and his enemy, obviously calculating something.

"Ah, but you'll be dead long before me, Flores."

Not if she could help it. "Oh, just smoke the damn thing," she managed to say through a tight throat, imitating Marco's flip tone.

"How kind of you to allow me one of the few gustatory pleasures I still have." He bowed mockingly at her. "Unfortunately I lost my sense of smell years ago. Occupational hazard."

"Cooking drugs in jungle labs will do that." Marco jerked his chin, motioning to the chaise. It was a solid Victorian piece, the heavy hardwood frame covered in thick upholstery. Maybe it could block some of the explosion sure to come.

But Marco didn't have any protection. All of her papers, canvases and paints were tinder for the flames. Marco would be unable to escape.

The bile rose in her throat. Time slowed as Rodríguez's hand settled on his gold lighter. She saw every ridge on the striker wheel pass under the flesh of his thumb. The heavy wood dug into her back as she scooted her feet under her. The flint sparked. For an agonizing moment Rey saw the turpentine fumes shimmer around the drug lord.

"Now, Rey!" Marco shouted. A flash of orange flame engulfed the man who called himself *El Lobo*. She threw herself onto the chaise and somersaulted behind it. She crashed hard on her right shoulder, her bound hands unable to break her fall.

The older man let out a long, hideous scream that raised the hair on her neck.

"Get out, Rey!" Marco's beautiful face was reddened from the explosion, his hair and eyebrows singed. He rolled to his side and tried to scoot himself to the loft's heavy sliding door.

She struggled to her feet, ignoring her painful shoulder. She tried to free Marco, but the tape had tightened from his struggles and she couldn't find the seam. "Hold on!" She flipped him onto his stomach and grabbed his calves with her own bound hands. She was grateful that adrenaline and years of hauling heavy stone blocks gave her strength to lug his helpless body to the door. She threw open the door and dragged him outside. He gasped as his injured ribs bumped across the threshold, snowflakes landing on his reddened skin.

An animalistic howl rose above the fierce winter wind that whipped up the flames. She turned to see Rodríguez rolling in agony, beating at his fiery legs and chest. He lit a pile of sketch pads on fire with his frantic moves. If she didn't put out the fire, he'd light her whole loft ablaze.

"Rey, you don't have time! The bullets in the guns cook off when they get too hot!" Ignoring Marco's shouts, she fumbled for her small fire extinguisher and pressed the lever.

She sprayed the burning papers and turpentine puddles before turning to the man who'd held them prisoner and planned to kill them both. She couldn't just leave him to burn to death in her home. Despite what he'd tried to do, no one deserved that. Well, maybe *he* did. But she wasn't going to have any dead-guy vibes in her home. She sprayed him with thick white foam, emptying the extinguisher on his miserable carcass.

She heard the wail of sirens from the fire station three blocks over. Thank God. They could deal with the mess. She only wanted to free Marco and make sure he was all right.

"Flores!" A terrible croak stopped her in her tracks.

She turned and saw Rodríguez had pulled himself to his knees. He lifted his gun in one shaking hand and pointed it at Marco, who was perfectly outlined by the streetlight. Marco stared at his enemy, his body bracing for the bullet's impact.

"No!" Rey screamed. The berserker blood of her Viking ancestors roared through her veins. She kicked his wrist. He screamed and dropped the weapon as his bones crunched under her toes. "That's for trying to kill us!"

Oil paints on a smoldering canvas burst into flame, but she ignored it. She aimed a kick at his stomach. "That's for hurting my sculpting arm." The orange flames and the ancient bloodlust turned her vision red.

She pulled back her foot once more. "And that's for Marco's *mamá* and all the other women you hurt!" Her sneaker sunk satisfyingly into his balls as he screamed and toppled to the floor.

The firefighters rushed by her as she ran to Marco. The paramedics had already cut him free. He grabbed her in a desperate embrace, each wrist still encircled with silver duct-tape shreds. "Why the hell did you go back? I told you the bullets cook off!"

"I don't even know what the hell that means!"

He closed his eyes for a second and kissed her hard. "It means they explode. You could have been killed."

"Oh." She shuddered, finally realizing how close they had both come to dying. She ground her mouth against his, her tongue tangling with his, inhaling his smoky scent.

The paramedic cleared his throat. "Hey, buddy, miss, we gotta check you both out. Not that you don't look like you're doin' okay, but them's the rules."

Rey reluctantly let go of him but wouldn't take her eyes off him, not even grimacing when the paramedic ripped the duct tape off her skin.

Some large men in dark suits ran up to Marco and started arguing with him. She tried to go to him, but the paramedic had her pinned down in the ambulance with a blood pressure cuff and an oxygen mask. She yanked off the mask. "Marco!"

He shrugged off the man in charge and hurried to her side. "Rey, these men are with DEA. They're not happy that I skipped out on them a few weeks ago, so I have to go with them now."

"Now? How did they even find you?"

"They followed Rodríguez to Chicago, but he gave them the slip. They had just about tracked him to your loft when all hell broke loose."

"We could have used some help." She gave the largest man an evil glance.

He came over to them. "Flores, if you don't move your ass, we'll cuff you and move it for you."

"You leave him alone, you asshole." She got off the stretcher, her knees wobbling. Marco steadied her.

Black Suit said, "I guess I don't have to ask what you've been doing while you were on the run, huh?"

"Shut up." Marco gave him a deadly look. "I said I'd go with you but only if she's protected."

"We'll take care of her. Let's go."

Marco released her reluctantly. "I'll call you as soon as I can. I love you, Reina."

"I love you, too." She stood alone on her street, emergency lights spinning sickening blue-and-red swirls on the neighboring buildings. The firefighters brought out Rodríguez on a gurney.

She turned away from the destruction of her home and let the paramedic wrap her in a scratchy blanket. "It'll be okay, ma'am, you'll see," he reassured her.

She shook her head. It wouldn't be okay until Marco came back and she was in his arms again.

20

REY WAS STRAIGHTENING her desk. It always had to be clean before she began an important project. The clean space helped clear her mind. The disaster-restoration service had removed all the smoke and fumes from her working area and had scrubbed the mortar between her antique redbrick walls. The workers had even installed a central vacuum and ventilation system. She thought her father must have paid for it, because the insurance wouldn't have covered the cost.

He and her mother had come home early from their extended vacation, fussing over her for the past several weeks. Rey's mother had dropped her usual self-centered attitude and had focused on her daughter. After a few mother-daughter talks, Rey thought her mother finally understood how important her art career was.

And here was the next step in her art career—the block of marble for the Stuart commission. Fortunately the stone hadn't been delivered until after the clean-up. She hated to think how the soot would have damaged its pure whiteness.

She picked up a head shot of Marco. No, make that Francisco, his younger brother. That mystery was solved. She pitched the photo into her wastebasket.

She had filed a few more invoices and thrown away some old invitations to gallery openings when she found the letter from the mortgage company approving her loan. Her hefty down payment as well as the new commissions that Evelyn had found had impressed the lender. According to her agent, there was no such thing as bad publicity. Several days of Local Artist Fights Off Insane Drug Lord headlines and TV stories had boosted her name recognition and the value of her artwork.

The letter read, "Congratulations for many happy years in your new home!" Funny, she wasn't very happy, even though she had her new mortgage, had tons of work and even got a thank-you phone call from the federal attorney in Miami, sounding almost gleeful to have his case "settled out of court," as he'd put it. She was also relieved that Rodríguez had the uncharacteristic decency not to die in her loft, instead succumbing to his injuries at the Loyola University Medical Center Burn Unit a couple hours later. She wasn't superstitious, but who wanted to take a chance on evil spirits? And if there was evil in the world, that old bastard had been its embodiment.

But it had been a month since the other federal agents had rushed her lover away. She had feared for him until she'd found a short article on the *Miami Herald* Web site detailing how Marco's testimony and evidence had brought down the rest of Rodríguez's drug smuggling operation.

She hadn't heard a single word from him since. If he couldn't dial a phone by now, he probably never would.

The marble block sat on a tarp. Rey blinked back moisture. The stone dust must be irritating her eyes. She got up from her desk and circled the marble, examining the pure whiteness faintly streaked with creamy brown mineral veins.

She remembered the explanation that Michelangelo had written to an admirer who had wondered how he did his sculptures: "I saw the angel in marble and chipped until I set her free." She tipped her head, trying to see Marco in the untouched stone. He was no angel, but with his help she had chipped herself free from her fears. Fears about her past, fears about her art, fears about her own sexuality and passions.

And now it was time for her to chip her statue free and maybe chip Marco out of her heart. If her heart cracked in two, well, it wasn't made of marble. It would heal. Eventually.

She chose her favorite cold-tempered two-inch steel chisel, kissed it for good luck, and raised the mallet for the first blow.

21

MARCO WALKED THROUGH THE French doors of the Stuarts' brand-new Roman rotunda and stopped to stare at the ten-foot-tall statue of himself. Actually Mars, the god of war, shield and sword at his feet. Rey had done a magnificent job, even using his short haircut. It looked just like him. Except for the fourteen-inch penis. Oh, well. As his beautiful Reina had said, who wanted trouble walking?

He'd already had enough trouble the past three months. Trouble sleeping at night. Trouble breathing when he thought of her during the day. Trouble getting his heart to start beating again when he saw a tall blonde and thought for an instant that it was her.

He wandered through the throng of guests celebrating the statue's grand unveiling and found its creator in the hallway leading to the private bath. The sight of her knocked the breath out of his lungs, reminding him it had been three long months since he had kissed her goodbye on the snowy street in front of her scorched loft.

Rey wore a sleeveless pale pink dress made from some material that floated around her trim thighs and calves. Its V-neck dipped low between her high, full breasts, highlighting her creamy skin. God, she was even more beautiful than he remembered, her pale golden hair piled on her head, pink cheeks flushed. A silver necklace with pink stones couldn't compete with the sparkle in her eyes. Her face glowed with excitement as she spoke with her friend Annike from the Swedish museum. He watched her, drank her in, until her friend walked away.

He came up behind her. "Hello, Reina." The words came out huskier than he'd expected.

Rey spun around at the sound of his voice. Her blue eyes flashed dangerously when she saw him. Her full rosy lips opened and closed silently. He wanted to kiss her but knew he had some explaining to do first.

"Marco." She didn't look glad to see him. All the color drained out of her face. "What are you doing here?"

"Your agent told me where to find you. The Stuarts were happy to send an invitation to the model for their new magnificent statue."

She pointed to the door. "Now that you've seen it, you can leave."

"I need to talk to you, Reina." Oh, God, he didn't know what to do if she didn't hear him out, let him ask for forgiveness.

"Now's not a good time, Marco. I have to mingle with people." She stared blindly past him, her breasts rising and falling rapidly.

"Please, *corazón*," he began.

"Corazón?" she parroted. "What does that mean anyway? Does it mean 'gullible artist who actually thought her male model was something special'? Or does it mean 'woman who hasn't heard from you in three months and didn't know if you were alive or

dead'?" Her voice broke on the last word and she stepped back, bumping into a waiter carrying a tray of empty champagne glasses.

Marco winced and steadied her. "It means 'sweet-heart.' I'm so sorry I couldn't call. I had to go to a safe house until the agency dismantled the rest of *El Lobo*'s organization."

"Save it for some other sucker, Mr. Model." She leaned in, her eyes glittering like blue ice. "Francisco's agent wants to sign you as a client. She was practically coming in her pants when she saw my photos of you."

He noticed a few heads turning at her rising voice and tugged her into a palm-screened alcove. "I'm not going to be a model. In fact, I don't even work for DEA anymore."

"Did they fire you, too?" she jabbed.

"They don't have much use for an undercover agent who's had his picture printed in major newspapers. Rather than ride a desk, I've taken a job with a private company that provides security advice for U.S. Customs."

"Congratulations. Now go back to Miami." She turned to leave.

He put his hands on her shoulders and leaned in, his lips only an inch from her creamy neck. "I can't. My job is near O'Hare Airport."

She stiffened. "Why stay here in Chicago? You've been chased, shot at and almost burned alive here. Miami's probably much safer for you."

"Because the woman I love lives in Chicago and would never leave her fantastic loft studio."

"The woman you love?" Rey couldn't believe what he was saying. How could he have left her for so long if he loved her?

"Reina, I must admit something." He sighed and ran a hand over his head. His hair had grown back from where the turpentine explosion had scorched it. He looked wonderful. He looked miserable. Good. "One reason I didn't call as soon as I should have is because I was ashamed."

"Ashamed?" She wasn't expecting shame. She had expected, *Honey, I was busy saving the world from narco-terrorism* or even *Honey, I was busy wrestling alligators in the Everglades* or worst of all, *Rey, I found a new lover and don't want you.*

"Yes, because of my pride, my desire for vengeance, I brought destruction to my mother's house and your loft. Destruction to *mi familia,* which means everything to me. But most of all, you."

"Me? I'm just fine." Just fine, except for a heart that had shattered like an alabaster vase dropped ten feet onto concrete.

A muscle jumped in his cheek as he met her eyes. "He hit you, bound you, would have raped you right in front of me, and I was powerless to stop him."

"What do you have to be ashamed of? You did your job, that horrible man is dead and you saved my life."

He barked a bitter laugh. "No, Rey, you saved my life. I was trussed up like a Thanksgiving turkey and would have roasted in the fire if you hadn't dragged me outside."

She lost patience with him. "The only reason you were tied up was because you threw down your gun to keep Rodríguez from killing me!" Unable to stand still any longer, she turned her back to him. "So you didn't call me for three months because of your stupid Cuban machismo?"

"Not machismo." He put a gentle hand on her shoulder and turned her to face him. "It's ironic. The Spanish words for *vengeance* and *shame* are almost identical. *Venganza* and *vergüenza*. I volunteered for undercover work because of my desire for revenge. For thirteen months I became one of them, watched them smuggle drugs, watched them kill people. I had such hate in my heart."

"It was your job. If you hadn't seen them do all those horrible things, you wouldn't have been able to testify against them."

He leaned closer. "I rejoiced in the killing of the other drug dealers." His voice was a gritty whisper. "My *papá* would be ashamed of me."

"Oh, Marco." She grabbed his clenched fist. Slowly he relaxed his fingers enough to entwine them with hers.

"Since they released me from protective custody, I have been working on my mother's house, which Rodríguez firebombed as soon as he realized who I was." He shrugged, his broad shoulders moving up and down in his navy blazer. "Doing the rehab by myself is only a small penance, but I have done my best to make it up to my mother and you."

"Wait a second. My loft has a new central vacuum and ventilation system. Do you know anything about that?"

A ruddy flush crept up his tanned neck. "You told me once that you wanted a central vacuum more than anything."

"Not more than anything! You! I wanted you more than anything!" She added a couple Spanish insults. *"Idiota! Pendejo!"*

His eyes widened. *"Querida,* where did you learn that?"

"My neighbors. And don't change the subject." She made a fist with the hand he wasn't holding and shoved his chest, pushing him against the wall she'd faux-painted to look like pink marble. "You left me for eleven weeks and four days and thought a vacuum cleaner would make it up to me?"

"No, I never thought that. But maybe this will." He cupped the nape of her neck and captured her mouth with his. His warm, soft lips weakened her knees until he wrapped his arm around her waist to catch her. All the loneliness, passion and love that had built up in her since she last saw him bubbled into a great geyser. She didn't even realize she was crying until he lifted his head.

"Oh, *mi amor,* my love, don't cry." He gently wiped away her tears with a thumb. She reached up and brushed the damp tracks left on his cheeks from her own tears.

She sucked huge gulps of air between sobs. "At first I thought you were dead. Then I thought you didn't love me anymore. And God forgive me, I don't know which made me cry harder."

"Oh, God, Reina. I'm so sorry." He blinked rapidly, and she realized he was as overwhelmed as she was. A tear spilled down his cheek and she caught it with her fingertip. He stared at her hand. "I haven't cried since I left Cuba on that raft."

"Marco." She threw her arms around his neck, their wet cheeks sliding across each other as she kissed him hungrily. He grabbed her bottom and lifted her against him, her thighs settling eagerly against his growing erection. He left her mouth to trail kisses along her neck and between her breasts. He nuzzled down her organza-covered belly until he was on one knee in front of her.

"When I promised to come back to you, I promised something else, as well." He pulled a small Tiffany aquamarine box from his jacket pocket.

She gasped as he took her left hand in his.

"You know I wanted to ask you before but wouldn't until we were out of danger. Well, the only danger left is to my heart if you don't say yes." He cleared his throat and popped open the box. "Rey, *mi reina,* my queen, will you marry me?"

She ignored the outstretched box and dropped to her knees so they were eye to eye. His warm golden gaze drove away the chill that had frozen her for the past eleven weeks and four days. "Yes, of course I'll marry you." She grabbed him and kissed him until he finally pulled away.

"Are you sure?" He laughed. "You haven't even looked at the ring." He held it up in front of her, the large round diamond shining like a star in the platinum band.

"It's beautiful." She slipped it on her ring finger and turned it so the gemstone caught the light.

"The diamond is set flush so you won't catch it on your art projects." He snapped the box shut.

"Perfect." The ring was perfect and so was he, so she kissed him again. "We have to find my parents and tell them."

"They're here?" He looked around nervously, no doubt expecting her father to descend on him in a berserker rage.

"Won't they be surprised to meet you!" Her father would be polite but a bit frosty to the man she'd cried over, and her mother would just look knowingly at the ten-foot naked likeness of him and congratulate her. Rey caught his hand and dragged him out of the alcove.

"And after I meet them, we'll go to Miami to meet my *mamá*. She has lots of comfortable poolside furniture."

Rey lost her breath at his sexy grin, wanting to drag him into the alcove and have a private engagement party. "Will you take me there?"

Marco caught her innuendo and kissed her new engagement ring, his hot breath tickling her skin. "Here, there, anywhere. Because I am yours and you are mine."

"Forever," she promised and took her new fiancé to meet her parents under the gleaming white statue. Her hands had created its beauty, but their love would create something even more beautiful. A life together.

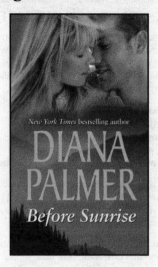

2 FREE

BOOKS AND A SURPRISE GIFT!

We would like to take this opportunity to thank you for reading this Mills & Boon® book by offering you the chance to take TWO more specially selected titles from the Blaze™ series absolutely FREE! We're also making this offer to introduce you to the benefits of the Mills & Boon® Reader Service™—

- ★ FREE home delivery
- ★ FREE gifts and competitions
- ★ FREE monthly Newsletter
- ★ Exclusive Reader Service offers
- ★ Books available before they're in the shops

Accepting these FREE books and gift places you under no obligation to buy, you may cancel at any time, even after receiving your free shipment. Simply complete your details below and return the entire page to the address below. You don't even need a stamp!

YES! Please send me 2 free Blaze books and a surprise gift. I understand that unless you hear from me, I will receive 4 superb new titles every month for just £3.10 each, postage and packing free. I am under no obligation to purchase any books and may cancel my subscription at any time. The free books and gift will be mine to keep in any case.

K7ZED

Ms/Mrs/Miss/Mr ....Initials ....

BLOCK CAPITALS PLEASE

Surname ....

Address ....

....

....Postcode...

Send this whole page to:
UK: FREEPOST CN81, Croydon, CR9 3WZ